USA TODAY BESTSELLING AUTHOR

Dale Mayer

TERKEL'S TEAM SERIES
WADE'S WAR

BOOK 02

WADE'S WAR: TERKEL'S TEAM, BOOK 2
Dale Mayer
Valley Publishing Ltd.

Copyright © 2021

ISBN-13: 978-1-773365-12-1
Print Edition

Books in This Series:

Damon's Deal, Book 1

Wade's War, Book 2

Gage's Goal, Book 3

Calum's Contact, Book 4

About This Book

Welcome to a brand-new series from *USA Today* best-selling author Dale Mayer, where dark-ops SEALs have special senses and skills, needed to solve intrigue, betrayal, and … murder. A series with all the elements you've come to love, plus so much more, … including psychics!

Sophia met Wade a few years back, and the last she heard from him was he'd be back to take her out to dinner—and never saw him again. Having spent several years in the meantime working with Merk and his team in Texas, when Terk called for her help, Sophia jumped at the opportunity to go. Even if Wade didn't get it, she knew a connection worth trying for when she felt it.

Wade is weak, helpless, his abilities damaged, after the attack on Terk's team. Seeing Sophia, the woman he fell in love with at first sight, is a sock to his gut. His defenses are already down, and he knows it will be impossible to keep her at arm's length a second time.

Wade must bring her closer, protect her, especially after their team was shattered from the initial attack, and subsequent attacks haven't eased—not with the world slowly realizing that not just Terk survived the attack but so did a few of his team …

Sign up to be notified of all Dale's releases here!
https://smarturl.it/DaleNews

PROLOGUE

WADE SIMCO WANDERED the small space. "Why are we in here? The place is empty." He turned to look at Terk.

"We're here," Terk replied, "because this concrete room is reinforced with steel. We need to build a tunnel to get out, but to also stop anybody from coming in."

"You really think it's that Iranian group we hunted down who's attacking us? But we thought we got them all?"

Terk nodded. "Like they thought they got all of us."

Wade shook his head. "I don't see how anybody could have survived our attack. Didn't you have Tasha checking that angle?"

"She's still working on it, that will take some time. But the Iranian group could have been training a shadow crew for all we knew. And I don't know anybody else with the same skills," he stated. "Didn't your brother train over there?" At Wade's silent nod, Terk added, "So, considering that, maybe Iran is our best option."

"I got it," Wade said, hating to hear his brother even mentioned at this point. Anger warred with grief and the lost future where they could have found a way to bury the hatchet between them. "But damn."

"I know. I know," Terk agreed. "And we need more people. Merk is bringing in somebody else to help with communication."

"What about Tasha?" Wade asked.

"Oh, we definitely need her, but we also need somebody else to help Tasha and us. According to Merk, this person is really good."

"Have you ever worked with him before?"

"*Her.* No, I haven't, but I trust my brother. It's somebody he has known for a long time, although he did say that she had worked for the team but more as a freelancer."

"That sounds dodgy."

"Well, in my experience, hackers tend to be that way," he noted.

"Yeah, that's true enough. Look at Tasha," he murmured. "I can't believe she and Damon finally got together. I've been bugging him about that since she first joined us."

"Yes, I think we all have. But at least he's finally getting it right."

"I'm happy for him," Wade muttered.

"So am I. They'll be good together," he agreed.

"And now that we have them together, the problem is, how to keep them safe."

"Right." Terk nodded. "And that's partly why we're bringing in another operative."

"Got it," Wade replied.

Terk cocked his head. "As matter of fact, they should be here any moment."

"Great. Do I know her?"

"I don't think so," Terk said, "but I could be wrong." He looked over at Wade and asked, "How are you handling your brother and all?"

"It's a sad thing," he replied, "but I always figured my brother would end up dead on a job one day. It's just some people always want to be on the wrong side of life. They don't give a shit about anything but themselves, and that was my brother. I loved him. I really did. But, in the end, I couldn't save him."

"And that's good enough for me," Terk said. "Nothing's easy about family, particularly if you're on the wrong side of things when it comes down to the end."

"No, not easy at all. He's gone, and—unfortunately or maybe not—maybe I'm grateful that my mom is also gone, so she didn't see what happened and didn't have to deal with the fact that we don't have a body to bury," he murmured.

"No, and I'm sorry if that's an issue."

"It isn't. My brother probably would have preferred this in a way. As sad as it seems, I think he would like to be a ghost in the world."

Just then Terk straightened. "We have company." He walked out into the other room as a *click* came at the door, and Merk walked in. But Terk's gaze was drawn to the woman at his brother's side and how her energy zinged right to Wade. Terk was surprised because he hadn't seen a foreshadowing of that happening at all.

Merk smiled. "And this is Sophia. Sophia Dermont."

Sophia stepped forward, looked at the men in front of her, then frowned when she saw Wade. "*You,* I know," she snapped.

He stared at her, as a grin crossed his face. "Well now, isn't that fun." He looked over at Terk. "We knew each other a while back."

Terk looked at him. "Knew?"

He shrugged. "Knew in the biblical sense. Not the long-term sense but we were a thing for a while."

The woman snorted. "I think the last thing out of your

mouth was, 'See you later.'"

"Sure, and here I am. It's later."

"Are you?" she asked, and she glared at him. "You were supposed to come for dinner that night."

"And then I got called to a job," Wade said easily. He looked at Terk. "She's your new hire?"

Terk turned to his brother. Merk nodded. "She's hell-bent for whatever sounds like technology."

Wade nodded. "And that's how we hooked up. We were at a seminar."

"Yeah, they didn't know anything there." She shook her head.

"We both had the same opinion."

Just then another door opened, and Damon came out, walking very slowly, Tasha at his side.

Tasha took one look and said, "Sophia?"

Sophia's face lit up, and she came running. The two women hugged each other, and Sophia whispered, "Oh my God, there you are. All the others are talking about what you did."

"I know. I'm very lucky that I survived," Tasha replied. "We're hunting those who tried to take us out."

Sophia looked at Merk and asked, "Is this true?"

Merk nodded. "Terk's team here was the target. He and Damon have been trying to piece things together. Wade was one of the casualties. He's only barely back. In fact, he woke up from a coma just a few days ago."

She turned her concerned gaze to Wade.

He shrugged. "I'm fine."

She nodded. "Good, then I can kick your ass later."

He grinned and said, "You can try."

"Count on it," she snapped, "and I'll win too." She

walked over to Terk, reached out a hand, and, when he placed his in hers, she studied Terk for a long moment. Everybody in the room could see the energy rise up ever-so-slightly. "Fine." She nodded. "I'm in."

"We can't have you come in and then walk out," Terk murmured. "This has to be a 100 percent commitment. We have to know that we can trust you and that you'll have our backs."

She looked at Terk and frowned. "It's only because you don't know me that I'll allow you to say that. After this moment, you don't ever get to misjudge me again. When I say, *I'm in*, then I'm in. Done deal." She looked over at Wade, frowned at him. "You and I, however, still have a score to settle."

He nodded. "Maybe. I'm looking forward to it. And welcome to the team."

She smiled, looked around at Tasha. "Now I feel better. This is a family I do know, and I'm more than happy to help out."

And, with that, she looked at the equipment set up in the main outer room and asked, "So, where do I start?"

CHAPTER 1

W ADE COLLAPSED ON one of the two beds in his new bedroom. They had moved out of their temporary headquarters in Paris and now were in this massive compound in the outskirts of Manchester, England, and Wade had no idea how Terk had found it. He'd apparently been tipped off by Bullard, somebody who worked closely with Levi.

However Terk found it, Wade was just damn thankful to have some privacy and a safe place to get his mind wrapped around what just happened. Only here, when he was alone, could he completely relax and unwind. Only after he was alone would he let his body shiver and shake with the pain of remaining vertical, trying to stay cognizant of everything going on around him. If his team had any idea how much Wade was still suffering, not a one of them would let him out of bed yet.

No way in hell would Wade get shut out at this point.

To think some of his teammates were still comatose was enough to make a grown man cry. They'd been good together, all of them brothers-in-arms, fighting the good fight the best way they knew how. "None of them deserved this shit," Wade muttered. He knew full well that nobody else in the industry would give a crap either, due to the kind of work they did and the type of life they led.

It was all fine and dandy, until everything blew up in your face, until you were forced to recover with absolutely no idea what the future would look like when the dust settled. Wade was a lot of things, usually fast on his feet, but these last couple weeks were on a different level. Not just a couple weeks in terms of recovery but things had gotten a little funky before the attack on his team.

He'd mentioned it to Terk once, but they were interrupted, and Wade hadn't taken the time or the effort to get back to his boss. Wade seriously regretted that right now because, if ever a time should have had clarity, that time was long past. As he lay here, trying to get his body to relax, a knock came at his door. He pretended to be asleep, hoping whomever it was would go away. When the knock persisted, he groaned and called out, "What's up?"

"Let me in."

He swore under his breath. That was Sophia, and one thing he knew was that she wouldn't be pushed around. He called out again, "Stop the damn knocking and come in, even though I need time and space to recuperate."

She opened the door, poked her head around, and then frowned. "Are you okay?"

"Of course I'm not okay," he snapped. "I came in here for a reason."

She hesitated and then walked in anyway. She was a one-of-a-kind person, full of life, spirited, and she didn't give a crap about petty shit, always riding on a chariot regardless. As she got closer to the bed, she tried to study his face, but he refused to turn toward her to let her get a better look. He didn't know if she had any abilities or not, but, as far as he was concerned, she was way too disconcerting on so many levels.

He had a reason for not contacting her again after the night they'd spent together—because he knew he couldn't get into a relationship with somebody like her. She was too perceptive, and his life was too secretive. Not a good combination. The last thing he needed was more chaos in his life, but he'd also been a coward and had decided that, since they had both arrived at the IT seminar with no commitment, he would leave the same way. That didn't mean she would accept it though.

"Do you want me to go get anybody?"

"Hell no. I would shoot you if you did," he replied quietly. She sat down on the side of his bed, making it bounce a bit. Instantly he winced.

She gasped. "Jesus, Wade. You didn't tell me it was that bad." A hint of hurt was beneath her concern.

"I haven't talked to you. Have I?" he asked, trying to hang on to his temper.

"Yeah, I was hoping to speak to you about that," she replied. "Maybe this isn't the right time."

"There's never a right time," he muttered.

"No, maybe that's true. I would like an explanation though."

"An explanation of what? Why I didn't call? That's easy. Because I didn't want to." He tried to avoid the snap in his voice, but it was hard. She knew the score as well as he did. They had made no commitments. It was just a dinner date after all, and he stood her up. At least that's what he kept telling himself.

"You know I was worried about you," she stated. "Did that not matter?"

"I got called out on a job, and it went to shit. As I recall, I got half blown up at the time," he muttered. "I don't even remember the details right now." He shut his eyes. "And that's just one of many that I've blocked. And I really don't want to bring them back." A long moment of silence followed, and he didn't even open his eyes because the small effort would hurt more.

"Is that really what happened?" she asked tentatively.

"As far as I can say, yes. I don't even remember anymore. I'm usually not the kind to forget unless there's a reason." He added, "And I had a reason, but, at this point, it really doesn't matter."

"Okay," she replied, "and I get that. I also get that you were probably in tough straits at the time. But that doesn't explain why you didn't call afterward."

"Too much time had passed, and it would have been awkward." *Just like the rest of my life,* he thought to himself.

"Do you really think that you're only allowed to have half-ass relationships?" she asked.

"They tend to work the best," he muttered.

She sighed. "You know what? I knew you would be work. I just didn't realize how much."

At that, his eyelids struggled to open up, and he stared at her. "This isn't about you."

"Of course it is," she muttered. "And I knew it at the time. I just had hopes that you would be … *easier,*" she noted, for lack of any better word.

"Well, I'd laugh at that if I weren't so exhausted. But why the hell did you ever think I would be easy?"

She gave him a half smile. "Obviously I was drunk."

"You think?" he muttered, letting his eyelids drop again. "Nothing about me is easy. Trust me on that."

"No, maybe not," she agreed, "but, at the same time, I also think you sometimes make things a lot more work than they need to be."

"Probably." He shrugged. "Did you have any other reason to bother me? I really could use some sleep."

"I can see that," she noted. "This isn't the first time I've seen you like this."

"Again, you don't know me," he muttered. "You don't know the shit I've been through."

"No, and there's a reason why I don't. Because you sure as hell haven't let anybody in."

After a long moment of silence, he finally nodded. "You could be right. Again, it's not the kind of life that works well for partnerships."

"Interesting that you didn't say that to me at the time."

"No, I didn't," he stated, "and, again, postmortems aren't my thing."

"So you want me to just get up and leave now, I suppose."

"Yeah, that'd be for the best." He still didn't open his eyes.

"Well, I'll have to think about that. But ... I don't think you'll get off that easy." Then she got up and walked out.

He didn't have a clue what to say. The fact was, she had offered something that he'd never really had before. Maybe it scared him. More than that, he knew just how dangerous his job was and how absolutely uncertain everything in his life would be. So to bring her, or anyone, into that kind of chaos was just not smart. So he had made a decision to walk away, and it troubled him that she wasn't listening.

He would have to deal with it later because he knew, for a fact, that she was damn good at her job and that they needed her skills in these unprecedented times. It just wouldn't be easy with her around because she was like a terrier with a bone. He didn't know why she cared so much, and the fact that he cared was something he'd kept well and truly hidden. She didn't seem to want to listen to any reason he offered. When a hard knock sounded on his door again, this time the door was pushed open without waiting for an answer.

Wade groaned out loud, exasperated. "I guess there's no such thing as privacy around here, is there?"

"Not when you're hurting."

Terk. Wade opened his eyes and glared at him. "Did she tell you?"

"Of course she did. Not only does she have whatever this ax is to grind with you," he noted, with a twitch of his lips, "but she cares." The twitch widened to a grin. "And the fact that she cares makes you a very lucky man, but you're currently not in a state to appreciate it."

"Of course I'm not," he muttered, shutting his eyes again. "Who wants to deal with that?"

"You, apparently." He smirked.

Wade shook his head. "She'll be a lot of trouble."

"Nope, she won't be," Terk argued, "but you might."

Wade opened his eyes and glared at his boss. "What's that supposed to mean?"

"It means that obviously she wants something … and you're it."

"Yeah, I know that." Again his eyelids fluttered closed.

"She doesn't seem the type to take no for an answer either. I'm surprised you're even fighting it."

"Why?" Wade asked in a flat tone. He waited for a moment, and then opened his eyes and glared at his friend.

"You know why," Terk said quietly. "You know perfectly well what I can and cannot see."

"Well, for once," he snapped, "you could just not tell."

"I can tell if I want to, but you do know that you're not being the easiest person to deal with right now."

"So what is this? My punishment?"

"No. It's hardly that," Terk stated. "And nobody who had caught Sophia's interest would ever consider it a punishment."

"Look. We hit it off. We had fun. Then I realized how deep it was getting and how much danger she would be in if we continued on the same pathway, so I called it quits." Wade made it sound like it was no big deal.

"Except for the fact that you're obviously not over her. Not even close. And she has that kind of energy that you could use to heal, and you're too stubborn to see it. It'll be a problem if she keeps you off your game."

"Well, you're the one who hired her," Wade snapped. "And don't go telling me now that you couldn't see the energy between us because you would have seen it in a heartbeat, if you'd looked." In frustration, Wade snapped his eyelids shut and tried to turn away from Terk.

"Maybe I didn't look," Terk admitted. "We were a little desperate, in case you don't remember."

Wade opened his eyes, turned his head, and stared at his boss, his friend. This discussion was getting them nowhere. So he changed the subject. "Anything new?"

"A lot," Terk muttered, "and none of it good."

"Speak up," he said, "and, if I don't have to move, all the better."

"I don't want you to move," he noted. "As a matter of fact, I might just bring a computer in here for you."

"I don't know if that would help or hurt. The noise out there, the energy, it's making me vibrate pretty badly."

"How are your senses doing?"

"At about 40 percent," he replied bitterly. "It's like walking around three-quarters blind, then getting blindsided in my own corner of the world."

"I get it. I'm sorry. Maybe I shouldn't have brought her on board, but, as I said earlier, we are critically short-staffed." Terk was truly remorseful.

"I know. I know." Wade groaned. "And, honestly, if I had the time and energy, I might have done things differently."

"Well, after this, you can do things differently," Terk replied, "because sometimes it's good to go with your heart."

"She doesn't need to know," he snapped, and a threat hung in his words. "I really won't appreciate anybody interfering." A razor-sharp tone filled his voice.

"Doesn't matter if you appreciate it or not," Terk replied, with an equally hard tone. "Anything that interferes with what we have to do becomes a team issue. We are all trying to hold it together with the small working team we have. I don't want a problem with you, and I need all you can muster," Terk murmured. "We're expending a lot of energy, trying to not lose any member of this team, and some are hanging by a thread."

"Okay." For the first time, Wade sounded uncertain.

"Take care of yourself," Terk said, "and I need you to pick up as much as you can—but not to the point that it puts you at risk. Get back on your feet, and let's see if we can find the asshole doing this."

"Yeah, sure. What do we have so far? And please tell me that it's not nothing." Terk was tired too. Wade saw that. It only made him feel worse.

"No, it's not nothing. We did find quite a lot, but we

just haven't found enough to nail down this shit."

"Is your brother still in the area?" Wade asked quietly.

"Yes, and I think he'll stay for a while. He's the one who brought Sophia."

"I'm surprised they didn't take her on over there. It sounds like your brother and Levi's team are always looking for more people." Wade was hoping to push her away.

"I think they asked her," Terk spilled, "but she declined, saying something about having some old business to settle."

Wade winced; he knew what that was. "She'll wage war against me, won't she?" he murmured.

"Probably. The question is, do you deserve it?" Terk asked. "Or want it?"

"I walked and never went back." Wade contemplated the situation. "It's not like we made any promises. We just hit it off, and she was expecting me for dinner, but I got called for a job, and that's when I got hurt a while back." He shrugged. "I didn't call her again. That's hardly an unusual situation."

"Yeah, but maybe take a good look at what you want now. Our lives, our priorities, all have changed."

"And what then? Get her sympathy?" Wade hated uncertainty. Hated being questioned. Even worse, he hated being judged.

"I don't know about sympathy, but maybe some understanding would resolve this mess between you two." Terk nodded. "I think she would appreciate it if you just told her the truth."

"Well, I'm not explaining our particular skill sets to her."

Wade was being a hard-ass, and Terk had no idea how to get him to see reason. He was working off emotions right now. So Terk just remained quiet, letting Wade stew in his thoughts for a moment.

"I could tell her a little bit, but I think it would just make her angrier that I was trying to hide out and to not get her involved."

"Yeah, it's funny how these women all seem to think that trying to protect them is almost a crime in itself."

"You're abso-fucking-lutely right there." Wade sighed and let his eyelids drop closed again.

"These women are tough, smart, and they don't appreciate being canceled out of the equation, Wade."

Terk had put a spin on the equation analogy to make his point, and Wade picked it up right away. It was not a bad way to let him know what he already knew—that Sophia was a spitfire.

"Sophia could serve your head on a platter." Terk chuckled. "She is independent, strong, and knows what she wants."

"And here I thought all the good women were gone," Wade mumbled. "That's what you told me a long time ago."

"Except now I'm starting to wonder if I was wrong," Terk muttered.

"What?" Wade jerked open his eyes to study Terk. Wade's earlier exhaustion had been somewhat diminished at the change of tone in his friend's voice. "What happened? Maybe you better bring me up to date. What the hell is this about?"

Terk hesitated. "It's not an easy story."

"Well, you can start at the beginning." Wade wouldn't let this go—not when interruptions had cost them an earlier very important discussion—and Wade had the time.

"The trouble is ... I don't know what the beginning is."

What came next was not what Wade had expected at all, ending with some poor woman in a coma, now carrying

Terk's child. "Jesus Christ." Stunned, Wade could only stare at him.

"Considering the fact that I've spent all my adult life making sure that I didn't get a woman pregnant," he stated, "it's pretty upsetting."

"Yeah, that's one word for it." What an insane turn of events. "When I was out of it, I was really out, wasn't I?"

"You weren't out long enough is the problem, as you are still hurting from coming back too soon." Terk shook off the effects of the conversation, standing straight. "I really would appreciate it if you would get yourself healed before you jump right back into this craziness."

"Well, if there wasn't such craziness," he replied, "it would be fine. If I can help, I need to help."

"Just so we're clear. It's not just you. I know that she needs to be protected, and everyone else on the team does too. "Trouble is, we needed people. We still need more people."

"I know. I get it." Wade added, "And I'm trying to be understanding of everything that's going on, but it's hard because I wasn't there, because I couldn't do anything about it."

"Remember. Everything has to happen in a certain way, and, unfortunately at this point, it feels very much like things will still blow up." Terk was clearly exhausted.

"You think?" Wade's question was interrupted by a series of alarms.

Terk muttered under his breath, then disappeared out the door.

Listening to the chaos going off around him, Wade had no idea if he should get up or not. He knew that they were all capable, but he had no idea what the alarms meant. Then the alarms shut off, leaving everything eerily quiet for a second. He leaned back in bed with a sigh of relief, noting Terk had left the door open. Wade was mustering up the courage to get out of bed and shut it, when she stepped in; Sophia was nothing if not persistent.

She looked at him hazily. "Good thing you stayed where you were. It was a false alarm."

"I doubt it was a false alarm," he argued, "more like somebody tripped the wire as a test."

She nodded. "I wondered about that."

"Yeah." Wade sighed. "You pretty well have to assume that, when it comes to the team here. I don't know what's going on, but obviously we've pissed somebody off pretty badly," he noted.

"I think you've pissed off lots of people," she stated, "and you know what? Maybe that's not a bad thing because some of this has to come to a head in order to get it all purged properly."

"That's not as easy as it appears," he muttered.

"Nope, it definitely isn't. Maybe that's also why you shouldn't do it alone," she noted, and, with that, she turned and walked out again.

It seemed like his bedroom had turned into a highway, with everyone speeding through all day long—not something Wade appreciated. But just when he was about to go back under and finally get a bit of sleep, the alarms went off again. This time something was different to it, and the yells and curses coming from the next room told a completely different story.

Pulling on his reserves, he closed his eyes to send out a trace. His heart squeezed in terror. Maybe they found what they were looking for after all.

SOPHIA WAS REALLY no good at subterfuge. For her, life was all about living in the moment, stepping in with everything she had. She had determined a long time ago that she wouldn't mold herself to anybody's liking, and, in a world with so much abuse and so much negativity, she had her own way of doing things, and she worked hard to be who she was. She had never tried to fool herself into thinking that Wade would be here, yet she'd secretly hoped to see him again. But seeing him injured like this—mentally drained and spiritually low—she wasn't exactly sure what to do, to say, or even to feel. Predictably she'd come across too strong and too crass and had pissed him off immediately. But, then again, what else was new?

It was hard for her to hide her emotions and to keep them all bottled up inside. It was hard for her to be anything other than who she was, and usually she wore her heart on her sleeve. The fact that he'd stood her up and then had never called her had been a terrible blow to her ego. It wasn't just a bruised ego that she was worried about; she would get over herself. She was worried about him, and to find out he'd been badly injured on a job and possibly because he was distracted over her was just too much to handle. She got it, and she really did understand that these guys were all about honor, discipline, and duty to protect everyone, but they also had to protect themselves.

She wasn't most women, and she knew how to protect herself. She may have mushy feelings for a guy not willing to admit he cared, but she still had control over everything. She understood the need for *somebody* to stay home and to keep the home fires going, to look after a spouse or a family, but she didn't come from the same era that said all women must be at home.

She was different, no matter how reluctant she was to admit it.

In fact, she was a lot like Ice.

Sophia had done a couple jobs with Ice, but more as a consultant than an actual working member of the team. Sophia hadn't wanted to take on another position like that, at least not until she figured out exactly what she wanted out of her life and Wade. And that hadn't been all that easy to determine, and now she was even more confused.

Her personal struggles aside, facing two cyberattacks in a matter of a few minutes had both her and Tasha sitting in front of their computers, blocking out everything else, as they worked hard to unscramble whatever the hell was going on.

Tasha suddenly yelped, "Gotcha, you little bastard!"

Sophia immediately pushed over her rolling chair and was by her coworker's side. "What did you find?"

"It came in through this door." She pointed at the screen. "Crap! What's that doing there?" she muttered.

Sophia rolled back to her station to look at her screen, typing fast to close off as many back doors as she could. "We need to do a full test on this system."

"Why don't you try to hack in now?" Tasha suggested. "I haven't even had a chance to give you a log-in, so just hack in, and let me know what you find."

"*Oh-kay*. Fine by me." Sophia immediately began her assault, and it didn't take long for her to realize that Tasha hadn't disappointed. "No way to get in quickly," she muttered. "This will take time."

"But then they had a little bit of time because they had

plans in place," Terk suggested, leaning over her shoulder.

Sophia didn't feel threatened or in any way upset by his presence. Something was calming but also distinctly unnerving about having him this close. She nodded. "And they've taken whatever steps they needed to. But what was the purpose of these two attacks? What does it mean?"

"They're testing our system. They're phishing to see how good we are. They want to figure out how many people we have left and which people at that," he noted.

She looked up at him and frowned. "Isn't that dangerous for them to know?"

"Yes, for us. If you know the strength of your enemy," he murmured behind her, "you can make plans on how to weaken them."

"Well, we can't let them weaken anything," Sophia muttered. "This is starting to piss me off."

"You and me both," Tasha said beside her. "We've been through a lot with these guys already."

"I get that, Tasha." Sophia turned to her friend. "I'm sorry. If I'd known you needed help, I would have been here sooner."

"I know that." She nodded, glancing at her friend.

"Do we go on the attack or ..." Sophia trailed off, her attention now on Tasha, as she continued clicking her keys, frowning.

"I think a physical counterattack is already in progress," Tasha replied.

Terk looked at her sharply. "In Manchester?"

"Yes! And following the routes they've been taking, I'm pretty sure they're heading toward your brother."

"That would be good if they did," Terk agreed quietly.

Sophia gasped, turned, and stared at him. "What?"

He smiled. "I was hoping we could send them in that direction."

"Why?"

"Well, Merk and Damon set up a trap."

Sophia was not convinced. "But did you really expect the bad guys to get into our system this quickly?"

"Again, knowing the strength of your enemies allows you to better understand who they are," he muttered. "Am I happy about two cyberattacks? No. But it also means some other really good hackers are out there. And we need to prepare accordingly."

"Maybe," Tasha agreed bluntly, "but we're the best." She twisted a bit to look up at Terk. "So you set up your brother as bait?"

"No." He shook his head. "My brother offered to set himself up as bait. We needed information, and, in order to get that information, we needed to find somebody … anybody, to get answers from."

Tasha slowly nodded. "That's your department. I handle IT." And, with that, she pivoted around and went right back to tracing the cyberhack.

Both women turned to their computers, moving on from the discussion, since the hacking team had more pressing concerns at the moment. Sophia was lost in a way, her tenure short here, and working with Ice had been different. Sophia knew and liked Ice, but to even begin to tell Ice to watch out for a trap was foolish in the extreme. Except as a heads-up warning. "You'll warn them, right?" Sophia asked Terk.

"Already done," he confirmed. "I stay in close contact with my brother."

Sophia wanted to ask just what that meant, and it didn't

appear she would get the chance to privately ask Tasha if she knew. Finally Sophia shook her head. "Rather than tiptoeing around this, I'll just ask. Has Merk got some of the abilities you have?"

"If he does, he never has developed them," Terk murmured. "So it's generally understood that the answer to that question is no."

She pondered his wording carefully. *Generally understood* was the phrase that caught her attention. "That would be very unusual in twins. Wouldn't it?"

He gave her a ghost of a smile. "All kinds of things in life are very unusual in our world."

She half smiled. "That, sir, sounds like an evasive answer to me."

"Whatever works," he replied, with a shrug.

And Sophia understood because, when you got into this shit, there was just no joy for anybody. "I hear you," she muttered. "Now, would somebody just tell me what it is that we'll encounter?" Just then she noticed activity on her computer. "A visitor is in the system right now."

At that, everybody jumped into action.

Tasha immediately started a hunt to destroy, and she suggested to Sophia, "How about you try to track where the intruder is headed, and I'll see how they got into our system."

"I'll get Wade," Terk said.

What for? Sophia spun in surprise, but Terk was already gone. She glanced at Tasha, who was busy, her keystrokes fast and sure, as she tried to track down what was going on. "Maybe we could have a talk later," Sophia noted, typing as madly as Tasha. "I'm feeling distinctly at a disadvantage."

"That's okay," Tasha replied. "You won't get a ton more

information anyway. These guys are something else."

Sophia nodded. "It's hard to work with them if I can't figure out what's going on around me," she explained. "I trust Terk and the team. I just wish I understood more."

"Oh, I know, and I get it," Tasha agreed. "I'm feeling better about the whole deal now, but I admit that, a few days ago, I was in the same boat and not feeling very secure at all."

"And what's this about you and Damon?" It was the mark of a good hacker who could talk on other matters while trying to catch an active hacker in her system.

Tasha flushed and smiled. "Yeah, finally." She shook her head. "I've been waiting since forever."

"Well, that gives me hope," Sophia shared. "Are they all like that?"

"Like what?"

"Dense," she said bluntly.

And even though Tasha was working hard on tracking down the intruder's manner of ingress, she went off in peals of laughter. "Well, let's just say they're superprotective, and anytime we have any security issue, you'll be the first one they shut out, for your own good."

"Yeah, that won't go down well," Sophia muttered. "Been there and done that. I'm definitely not going for round two."

"Nope, it never does work, so you fight back as much as you can. Just save your battles for the ones that will do you some good."

Sophia thought a word of warning might be in there somewhere. She just wasn't sure and couldn't reply now as Terk came in hot.

"Both of you get off the system right now."

Tasha looked up at him in shock. "No! No … I'm almost there."

"Stop." His voice was razor-sharp, which made Tasha lift her hands off her keyboard.

Sophia frowned but followed suit.

"Fine." Tasha was irritated. "You know what? It would be nice to have some inkling as to what's going on."

"Ha! I thought we weren't allowed to ask questions like that," Sophia muttered under her breath, noting a weird hum filling the air. She shook her head, as if trying to get rid of the ringing in her ears. She looked over at Tasha to see if she had noticed it, but she sat quietly at her computer, waiting.

Sophia peered up and around to see what the hell Terk was doing, but it seemed he was waiting as well, his head cocked to one side, listening to something in the air. She took a slow deep breath. "Somebody will have to explain some shit to me at some point," she announced.

"If and when," Terk replied, and the next moment he was out of the room.

Sophia looked over at Tasha. "If and when what?"

CHAPTER 2

TASHA JUST SMILED and gave her a lopsided grin. "Lots of things here don't work the way you might expect them to."

"Yeah, I can see that," Sophia muttered, "but I still don't know what the hell is going on."

"It's not my place to say anything," Tasha stated. "All I can tell you right now is that it could take some time to understand this team, but you will know soon enough. Just remember. Trust is a two-way street."

"Oh, I get that." She nodded. "I really do, but—"

Wade walked in. He stared down at her soberly. "It would be better if you went home."

Pain stabbed at her. "Yeah, well, that's not happening. Especially after seeing whatever the hell I just saw. What is going on here?"

He hesitated. "Just think carefully. It is not too late, and you can go home right now, where you'll be safer and where you can forget about all this shit, or else we'll turn the corner, and we'll be on yet another crazy job, and you'll be embroiled in it and at risk, whether you like it or not."

"Then bring it on," she snapped. "I'm not the kind to walk away."

"It would be better if you did," he repeated in a harsh tone.

"You can't scare me away like that," she snarled, almost growling. She was pissed off at herself and at him because he was being so damn stubborn. He did give a shit, and she knew it. She'd seen it—such depth of emotions and desires that she wasn't prepared to let him go without a fight. This wasn't a fight against her; he was fighting against himself. Against the two of them being together. And that just made her feel like she should hold on to him, at least for now. "So bring it on, McDuff," she snapped.

At that, Wade unexpectedly laughed. "Fine. Have it your way." He turned around to Terk, who hovered near him, protecting him in some way.

"Going to finish what you started?" Terk's tone was playful.

Wade looked at him. "I'll need a hand back to the bed, if you want me to do that."

"You got it," Terk replied, and, with that, he helped him into his bedroom while Sophia stared.

She lowered her voice to speak to Tasha. "How will getting him back to bed help us out of this mess? Finish what?" she muttered in confusion.

"That's just a part of this," Tasha answered. "I don't know if Merk told you anything, or if Levi or Ice or their crew ever talked about Terk's team, but the stuff that goes on here, it has an esoteric supernatural bent to it," she explained. "The remote viewers, the transmitters, trackers, cyberguards, and some of the tech here is kind of weird and wonderful. All psychic phenomena. You'll never find this shit anywhere else. Or at least we hope not. If you do find some of this anywhere else, then somebody found out about our guys' special skills, and they're using the same techniques on them again."

Just then yet another set of alarms went off, and, with a sigh, Sophia turned back to study the computers, only to find absolutely nothing flashing. She spun again to see Tasha bolting to her feet, yet going nowhere. She stared at her friend in shock, as Tasha just nodded slowly.

"Wade was badly hurt in this last attack that brought down the team," Tasha added quietly, "but right now he's the one chasing the bad guys on the ethers."

Bad guys ... ethers ... supernatural? "Holy crap, how did I miss that?"

"It's one of the reasons Wade is determined to keep you out of it," Tasha noted, "because so much can go wrong that is well beyond our physical abilities to fight." She sighed with a one-arm shrug. "I didn't understand it myself for the longest time. It took me quite a while to get into the actual swing of things, and even now it doesn't feel right."

"You think?" Sophia was clearly shocked. "That's all a bit hard to even grasp." She wasn't ready to accept any of it just yet.

"Speak to Terk if you have any doubts," Tasha suggested, "but you need to do it now because, once you commit, you cannot go back. Even now it might be too late."

"Too late?"

"I'm sure you can understand how we can't have anybody take off from here with this kind of knowledge."

"When they said, *top secret,* they didn't mean this," she replied with half a smile.

"Nope," Tasha replied.

"On the other hand, if I were to tell anybody, they'd set me up for a psych eval immediately."

"Yeah, except for the ones who *really* want to hear exactly what you could tell them in that psych eval," she whispered, "because this shit here is for real."

Bewildered, Sophia shook her head and didn't know what to do or say. "I mean, obviously I want to know more. I want to know everything there is to know because this is beyond anything I could have ever imagined."

"Beyond everything, but it is everything," Tasha noted. "That's the thing to remember. Even though it feels like it's beyond everything, this is the reality of where we're at."

"And somebody found out, then came in and attacked everyone?"

Tasha nodded. "And from there, it's gone straight downhill. If you consider the fact that our own government might have been the reason for the attacks"—she paused—"you might understand a little more."

"Well, I could actually understand that," Sophia replied, "because they'd be terrified of what your team could do."

"Hence the problem. We think the attack did come from our government, one way or another. But it's also my life on the line. I'm not prepared to just walk away and let them decide if I get to live or die," Tasha stated bluntly.

"No, of course not," Sophia muttered. "Jesus, what a mess."

"What a mess but also," Tasha added, with a smile, "like, *wow*. It's the wild part you need to hang on to because there's a lot of *wow* here. Like some *serious wow* stuff, but it also takes a fair bit to get your mind wrapped around it. Plus, then you have to understand that, when we're told to do something, we have to just do it—because we don't understand the implications from the other side."

"Like what Terk just did. Ordering us to stop, letting the hacker just proceed." Sophia shook her head at that. "And here we go down that whole *Alice in Wonderland* rabbit hole again."

"Exactly. He was letting Wade do his stuff in our system, so we had to stop. And it's not easy to blindly trust, especially when it comes to the IT part, which is our domain of expertise. I get it," Tasha agreed, "but you really do need blind obedience here because you don't know the whole situation at any given moment."

Sophia winced at that. "Like any job, someone must be in charge, and I don't have a problem with that, in theory." She laughed. "Except that I'm damn good at what I do, and I don't like people questioning my hacking." She shrugged. "I'm still trying to wrap my head around just the thought of all the team's cyberactivities and paranormal abilities. It really is a bit too much to take in, and, Jesus, if anybody got hold of this information—"

"Which is also why it's so damn important that they don't," Tasha replied. "And Terk and the guys are more vulnerable than ever, which is awful, especially since we're very limited in what we can do right now."

"I don't know about that," Sophia questioned, looking at her friend. "It seems like these guys have an awful lot they can do."

"They can, sure, but we have team members injured—some may die—and we still don't know anything about who attacked us. We've found one clue out of all this chaos," she noted, "but he's dead too."

"Of course he is," Sophia muttered. "Everybody will be expendable in this scenario. Aren't they?"

"Absolutely." Tasha was like Sophia, no BS whatsoever. "It's good that you got that right off the bat."

"Oh, I got it all right," Sophia agreed, "but, man, that's a really shitty thing to have happen. So, what can I do to help?"

At that, Tasha nodded slowly. "Right now, nothing for us to do. I'm just really glad you're here, but what we would normally do? We'd get leads. We get data." She reached over, the two women gripping hands.

"I don't know if you know," Sophia shared, "but Wade and I have a bit of history."

Tasha laughed. "Well, I got that message."

"I really don't want to see anything happen to him."

"Well, that's good," she agreed. "Then you'll do your best to help me keep the rest of them alive too. And, hey, since Damon and I finally got ourselves clear of all our misunderstandings, I would like to think that maybe we could help you two get through it as well."

"That would be nice," Sophia noted. "It's been pretty damn shitty, knowing that Wade walked. But now? Finding out that he did it to keep me safe? It seems even shittier somehow."

"Maybe, but it's how these men are built," Tasha stated. "You better just accept it and move on." She paused. "Remember. The best thing you can do is pick your battles, and, when they're here, the battles are pretty—" She stopped, hesitating. "They're pretty extreme, not always on our level. And that's just something else to deal with. But it's also fascinating in many ways, and they would say that we're capable of doing the same things."

"It's hard enough to believe any of this *ether warfare* even exists, without trying to take it to another level, thinking that we could do it too."

"Of course." Tasha nodded, with a smile. "But not everything is as simple as that."

"No, it never is, unfortunately." Sophia looked around.

"And, since I'm staying on with the team, I presume we need to stay here, at headquarters, for a long time."

Tasha nodded. "Where's your gear?"

"Back at the hotel."

"We'll bring it in later then," Tasha replied.

"Sounds good." Sophia hesitated, then looked over at Tasha sheepishly. "You're not kidding me, right? Wade really is in danger?"

"He barely survived one horrific recent attack," she stated, "and so have I. We lost the other two hackers—admins, like me. They were shot in their beds, while sleeping. It's a miracle that I heard somebody coming for me and had time to hide, so my bedding got shot up, instead of me."

At that, Sophia's eyes widened. "Jesus, and the rest of the guys on the team?"

"They're all still out of commission. Terk and Damon weren't hurt as badly, so they were okay enough to get started and to get me out. Of the rest, Wade is the only one of the others who has recovered to the point of being conscious and able to help."

"Okay, done deal. I'll get my stuff, and I'll move into one of the rooms here." She hesitated, then looked toward the bedroom where Wade was. "You know what? If I'm to start out the way I intend to go," she thought out loud, "I might as well just move in his room."

"You might want to wait until you get an invite first," Tasha suggested, with a smirk.

At that, Sophia's face broke into a broad smile. "Believe me. I don't need a proper invite. We were hell on wheels together."

"But he's fighting an awful lot of honor systems." Tasha frowned. "He may not take it well."

"And, if I let him get away with that," Sophia stated, "you and I both know he'll continuously balk at it."

"So, what do you want to do?" Tasha asked.

"Well, when I get my stuff," she stated, "I'll make my decision then."

"Good enough." Tasha shrugged. "But I'm kind of with him on this one."

"That's only because you don't know how much he cares," she suggested.

"No, I don't, and, maybe if I did know, it would change my mind."

Sophia nodded. "It'll be a little hard to see it, when he keeps me at arm's length."

At that, Tasha smiled and laughed. "This newest compound itself may be massive, but we are limited to just these few outfitted rooms—our operations room and the bedrooms and the kitchen-dining-conference room area. So where we actually live and work is a cramped and combined space, and it'll get more and more cramped as more of the guys wake up," she added. "Yet it's very much a whole integrated team at play, so, if you guys as a couple have problems, it'll affect all of us. And trust me. I found out the hard way. Terk won't stand for it."

"Got it." Sophia nodded. "That's a really valid point, and I'll think about it."

Terk silently entered the main room and gave a slight chin nod to Tasha. She returned the motion and waved Sophia back onto her keyboard.

They went back to fine-tuning their system and tracking their unwanted visitors. Tasha moved through the system and looked over at Sophia. "It feels different now."

"Yeah, it does."

Tasha added, "I suspect Wade went through here and did a cleanup."

Sophia sat back and had to bite her tongue. *What the hell does that even mean?* she wondered. *How could he have done it?* But it seemed to be completely normal to Tasha, so Sophia kept her mouth shut, or tried to, then mumbled, "I just need to learn more."

"You'll get there," Tasha said gently. "Just don't push it."

The trouble was, Sophia had never come up against something like this. And honestly? *Pushing it* was kind of her thing.

WADE WOKE UP what seemed like hours later, exhausted from fending off the cyberattack. He opened his eyes to find Terk at his bedside, sitting there quietly. "What happened?" Wade asked.

"You went after the cyberintruder."

At that, Wade winced. "Well, I tried to."

"Tell me. What happened?"

Wade searched his recent memories bank to see if anything was there, and then he sighed. "I have no idea."

"How are you feeling?"

"Pissed."

At that, Terk smiled. "And you know that I get that. I really do. It's not helpful, but I get it."

Wade wanted to laugh, but, at the same time, he wanted to scream and to shout. "I'm useless if I can't have my cybersenses fully back and if I can't actually track anything ..."

"I wouldn't say *useless*. You did something, even if you don't remember." Terk added, "As a matter of fact, I think something's very valuable in all this."

"And what's that?" Wade asked bitterly, "because I'm really not feeling it."

"No, you're not, but that doesn't mean it's not there. After we had two DOS attacks, you went in after them. I presume you did something in the computer system."

He frowned. "I might have, but honestly I don't remember."

At that, Terk frowned. "Are you saying you didn't get into the system?" he asked cautiously. "Because somebody cleaned the computers and put in a scrambler."

"Ah, yeah, I set that in motion before," he agreed. "I needed to do something to stop them from getting in."

"As long as that was you," Terk noted, smiling.

"Again, I hope so."

Terk chuckled. "I would prefer to have something more definitive, but I'll take that half-assed yes for the moment."

Wade reached up to scrub his face. "Yeah, you and me both. Jesus, I can't believe it's this bad."

"It'll get a lot worse if we can't get you back up again," Terk stated.

"You got any suggestions for that?"

"Well, getting some rest would be one," Terk answered, with a note of humor.

Wade rolled his eyes at that. Then he remembered Sophia. "Is Sophia still here?"

"She is working with Tasha, but I highly suspect she's planning on moving in. Now, if you don't want that, you need to tell me right this moment, and I'll put a stop to it."

Wade stared at him in shock. "Moving in *how*?"

At that, Terk's lips twitched. "I think you probably know exactly how."

"Oh crap," Wade muttered.

"I can see how much you care about her."

"I've always cared," he admitted. "It's rare to find someone so very much like you, someone you really want, but you know you shouldn't have." He shook his head. "It was for her own good that I walked away. You know that, right?"

"Well, if nothing else, we both know exactly how women feel about us telling them that."

He smiled. "And yet she knows nothing about this."

"Well, she knows a hell of a lot more now," Terk told him. "She was there in the computers when you did whatever you were doing."

Wade winced. "*Great*, so she must really think I'm a freak now."

"I don't think she would call you a freak. She's more fascinated."

"Well, *fascinated* isn't good either," he snapped.

At that, Terk started to laugh. "You won't get an argument out of me, so don't try to pick one."

Wade groaned. "Why is nothing ever simple?"

"It's not meant to be simple," he stated. "It's meant to be worthwhile, and they're not the same thing." At that, Terk stood. "Now you need to get some rest. Doctor's orders."

"*Great.* Oh … wait just a minute. I need to tell you something." He waited for the information to rise into his brain. Terk sat back down again and waited. That was the thing about Terk. If you needed time, he gave you time and never sat there impatiently or tried to push. It was way too important from his perspective that you got the right information. Wade nodded. "I got a name."

"A name?" Terk leaned forward. "That would be good news for a change."

"I don't know how much good news though. It was floating in my memory. But it means nothing to me." Wade frowned. "It's Lui Pul," he enunciated it carefully. "Give me a sec, and I'll see if I can get a spelling, not a pronunciation." Then he nodded and spelled it out, "L-U-I … P-U-L …

"Strange name."

"Yeah, it is, but that's how he thinks of himself. Unfortunately, I think, when it comes to dealing with people, they know him by another name."

"Well, that's pretty common in our business. I'm sure if we run a search for that—"

"We won't find anything."

"Maybe not, but it's definitely got a European bent to it. So they're using European talent," Terk noted. "That isn't a surprise in our global market. Could be local hires by the US government."

"Or could be local hires by the Iranian government."

Terk nodded. "We *are* dealing with a worldwide economy and staffing."

"Hell, could even be the Iranian government assisting our own government—a kind of *the enemy of my enemy is my friend* thing."

Terk sighed. "What people don't understand, they fear—whether our government or another." He paused, shaking his head. "Still the name itself is not much help."

"I know. Dammit, I was hoping I could wake with something really useful."

"It doesn't mean that you didn't," Terk noted. "It's just not enough yet."

"It's never enough," Wade growled. "That's the problem with this kind of work. It's just never enough. We do what we can, but we only get tidbits."

"Not true," Terk argued. "The stuff you were picking up before the whole team was attacked was amazing." Terk paused. "What we need is to get you back to that point again."

"And I don't know how to do that." Wade frowned. "I tracked that signature last minute, right before we were all downed. And honestly, I've been trying to find its spores, but it's been really hard to locate again."

"Did you see anything like that within our system? Was it in the computer or in the code?"

"That's the thing about tracking within electronics," he noted. "It's not the same thing as tracking on a physical realm. Everything changes and looks and feels differently at that level."

"So, is that a no?"

Wade frowned and then shook his head slowly. "No, it isn't a no. I'm not sure what it is yet, but I don't think it's a no. So there is a good chance it was *him*—that same signature I tapped right before we all got hit has now shown up today," Wade stated reluctantly. "I'm just not sure I can say that for certain."

"Got it," Terk murmured. "I want you to rest and then try hard to go back in again and see what you can come up with. But not until you've rested."

"That's not easy to do, like waving something in front of a bull and expecting us to calm down over it all."

"You'll do what you need to do because you have to," Terk murmured. "We all do." And, with that, he got up and headed for the door.

DALE MAYER

"Wait," Wade cried out.

"What?"

He frowned. "There's just ... Something's right there," he murmured. "I can almost feel it." Terk backed into the room and sat down right beside Wade. Terk just waited and waited, until finally Wade closed his eyes in dismay. "I can't get it."

"You will," Terk stated. "I have every confidence that you will."

"What if I can't?" he cried out.

Terk smiled. "Then we won't worry about it. You know as well as I do that we can't push what isn't there, no matter how much we may want to."

"It's hardly fair though. I feel like I'm dead weight."

"You're here. You're alive. And you're a damn sight more than what we had before. Now get some rest." And, with that, Terk was gone.

It wasn't exactly the most encouraging support Wade had ever heard, but he understood because it was true. They didn't have much info before, but now they had a name—or part of it at least. It's just wasn't enough, not yet. He closed his eyelids and tried to rest, hoping that the other information would slide up through his subconscious. It happened a lot of times that way, but, back then, he was whole. Now he was still so damaged.

When he opened his eyes the next time, he wasn't alone. Sitting in his room, whether he wanted her there or not, was Sophia.

She walked closer and sat down on his bed and picked up his hand. She whispered, "How are you?"

"Ask me later."

"I got it. Tasha said you were in the computer?"

He opened his eyes and then nodded. "Yeah, it was me."

"That was freaking amazing, but how?" she asked. "And since you did whatever you did, nobody has been back."

"Which is why I did it," he explained, "but it tired me out." He didn't explain what he did, why, or even how, and he could only hope that she would let it slide. Some things were just too complicated to explain. And the stuff his team did? Well, it needed to be parsed out in bits, or it could overload a person.

She patted his hand gently, and he relaxed, shifting on the bed. "You're still in a lot of pain?"

"Not so much. I was in a coma for a few days. Since I came out of it," he added, "everything has just been really taxing. Not the same. Senses, nerves on overload, that type of thing."

She hesitated before speaking. "I don't know anything about this stuff, but did they do something to you while you were in that coma?"

His eyes flew open, and he stared at her. "Like what?"

She winced. "I really don't know because I have no clue what we're talking about here," she admitted. "It just seems plausible to me that, while you were in such a vulnerable state, they might have done something."

"No … and the reason I can say that with any degree of certainty is because I know that Terk kept up security around us the whole time."

She stared at him and blinked. "Like the whole time? Guards and everything?"

"Well, not quite the security that you would imagine"—Wade grinned—"but someone was watching over me. Terk is pretty amazing."

"I know. I've heard … *things* from your team," she

shared, "but nobody ever really explains anything."

"That's because you're on a need-to-know basis. Terk doesn't involve himself very much with each of these scenarios, unless there's actually a problem, in which case he jumps in and warns the appropriate people. The team doesn't discuss our particular skills much, so a very limited number of personnel has access to substantial information."

"I can sorta understand that. The compartmentalization cuts down on who can find out what—not among us. In case we're caught. *Okay.* That rings true and makes sense now," she agreed. "When I was at Levi's place, one time Terk said something to Ice that worried her. She didn't go out that day, but I don't really know what was behind it all."

"You don't argue with Terk when he shares insights like that. He's just way too right too damn often."

"And that's kind of scary too," Sophia murmured.

"Very, but when you have somebody who can give you an inside scoop, you take it, and you make it work for you."

"Got it." Sophia nodded. "Do you want something to eat or drink?"

"As much as I want to say no, I probably should," he admitted.

"Well, feel like getting up? Or I can bring you something to eat. Any preferences for what you want me to get for you?"

He rolled his eyes at that. "I'm not an invalid."

"No, but you're exhausted, and, if there's anything I can do to help, I'm more than happy to."

And she had said it in such an honest way that he nodded. "Sorry, not trying to be a prick here," he apologized, "I'm just tired."

"And I understand that part." She sighed. "I might not

understand a whole lot about this, but I'm getting there. What I do see is an exhausted man whose reserves have been spent doing something that I couldn't help with, even if I wanted to. So, if getting you some food is in any way a help," she explained, "I'm happy to do it."

"Good luck with that. You'll probably have to fight Ta-sha for food."

Sophia chuckled. "Oh my God, does she still eat like a horse?"

"Two horses," he replied instantly. "Honestly I've never seen anything like it."

"She's beautiful inside and out," Sophia noted, with a smile. "We've been friends for a long time, and that is a friendship I value."

"It's a good thing," he noted, "because, when it comes to things like that, around here, our relationships are about all any of us have."

She nodded. "I really do understand that."

"Good," he agreed, "because it'll be tested. Everything you have ever believed will be tested. Then, when you finally think you've got it, it'll all get thrown up in the air, come back down as something completely different, which you may no longer recognize."

She stared at him, considering his words. "You know something? Life was getting boring before anyway. I'll go get you some food, and I'll come back as soon as I can." She stood and walked out.

Wade remained in bed for a moment, only to look over his room and see her bags. She really had brought them over, apparently waiting for him to say yes or no. He frowned at that, wondering if they could get past everything that had gone on before. Was there any reason not to go in that direction?

She was already here; she was already in danger, and, if he were honest, he didn't want her to be anywhere but here. With that, he got up and made his way to the bathroom. When he returned, he tossed her bag on the spare bed and laid back down again.

When she walked in a little bit later, she smiled at him. "Good news! Tasha didn't eat all the food, so I guess it's your lucky day after all."

"Glad to hear it." He yawned, chuckling at her cheekiness. "I'll tank up a bit, and then I need to drop again."

"Aye, aye, captain." She grinned and proceeded to bring over his meal.

He shifted on the bed, sitting up a bit, then looked up at her. "Did you bring some for you?"

"I'm not hungry," she replied easily. "Besides, I need to see that you get enough."

He frowned at that but realized that it really made the most sense, even though it sat wrong.

"Glad to see you're not arguing," she murmured.

"Well, I would if I were feeling better," he noted, "but really no point in arguing over something so obvious."

She smiled. "Good." Glancing over at her bag at the end of the second bed, she asked, "So does this mean yes?"

"Yes, what?" he asked, bringing the sandwich midair.

She looked over at him, smiled. "My bags."

"Yes, it's a yes. At least for the moment, while we figure out if this is what we want. At least this way I can keep an eye on you."

She hesitated and then slowly nodded. "Ditto."

When he realized what she meant, he shook his head. "You know that you can have a far easier life somewhere else, right?"

"I already told you that it's been boring. Remember? So just eat and shut up."

He burst out laughing, and, by the time he finished his food, he felt the fatigue hitting hard again. "I think I need to crash." He could barely keep his eyelids open.

"You need to because we'll need you soon," she noted.

"Why is that?" He yawned again.

"Because, without you at the helm here, we'll be more than a little shorthanded." He immediately bolted upright. "Merk and Damon are still out on their sting op?"

"Yes. They lost the guy in an underground parking garage. They'll sit there for a while, but, with just a partial crew, they can't stay there long."

He sat up, turning to throw his legs over the bed.

She shook her head. "Hell no, I shouldn't have told you anything until you had some sleep."

"But you did, and now I'm worried."

"Then you need to rest up to get back on your feet so we can utilize you," she stated. "You've got four hours, and then I'll wake you."

"But will you?" he asked in frustration.

"I promise," she stated calmly. "I know how important this is to you and to the team. So four-hour crash time, and then you're off on your own."

He smiled, nodded. "It's a simple test."

"And I won't fail you," she whispered, as he closed his eyes and sank back into the bed.

"Watch out for the next att—" he muttered inaudibly. Then he was gone.

CHAPTER 3

SOPHIA WALKED BACK out to the main room, finding Terk standing there, waiting, his hands on his hips. "I told him that I'd get him up in four hours," she said to Terk, knowing in some ways that gaze saw more than she'd ever understand.

"We, on the other hand, need to figure out what's going on and to make things a little bit clearer in terms of plans," he noted. "It would help a lot if we all got four hours." He was clearly on edge and exhausted too.

"Well, you for sure. Go ahead and grab your four." When Terk hesitated, she continued. "I've done lots of operations with your brother. You don't believe me, but you can check with him," she offered. "So take a leap of faith and get four hours."

He hesitated, looked over at Tasha, working on the computers.

"I'll work with her, and see if we can get ahead."

Terk nodded. "The systems are much more secure now after Wade did what he did, but we need to lockdown the computers and our new headquarters."

"Tasha's also running scenarios that I'm not really privy to yet." Sophia frowned. "It would help if I was, but again I'm not quite there yet. Just so much that needs explaining to me."

"And speaking of explanations"—Tasha rose and walked closer—"anybody got a problem with me filling her in?"

"No." Terk shook his head. "Sophia has to know. Although she might decide to leave as soon as she hears more," he teased, with a note of humor.

"I don't think so," Sophia noted. "I've thrown my lot in with you guys, even if only for the sake of having another go at Wade. But, once I'm in, I'm in. You go rest, and we'll figure out where this hacking bastard is."

"What makes you think he's even still around or will come back?"

"Something Wade said, as he dropped off." She frowned. "Something about *watch out for another attack.*"

Terk's eyebrows shot up. "Did he just say that?"

"Yeah, but he was falling asleep, so didn't expand on that theme. Personally, I'd expect the next attack to be physical."

"Which means we need to be prepared either way. I will be in my room, if you need me." With that, Terk left the operations room.

Sophia watched as Terk walked away and headed off to the bedroom at the corner. After a few seconds, she turned to Tasha. "Will he rest?"

"He'll rest as much as he can," she replied in a low voice. "Usually that's not very much."

Sophia frowned at that. "It's hard to continue doing this job at that same level if you never get enough rest," she murmured. "Especially right now, with everybody so shorthanded and under attack."

"I understand why they're doing what they're doing," Tasha admitted. "It's their protective instincts kicking into high gear. And, within the team itself, it's amplified even more. The team is family to them. You can't fight them from being themselves. Give them some leeway, a little bit of patience and tolerance."

"I get it." Sophia sighed. "It's the problem with being a geek. Once we do the computers, they do all the dangerous stuff, and, whether we like it or not, we're stuck watching and waiting for them to leave and to maybe never come back."

Tasha sucked in her breath at that. "Yeah, and I don't really want that reminder right now."

"Sorry, I didn't mean to make it sound quite so bad. It's just frustrating to watch Terk walk away, knowing that he will only get a minor amount of sleep because, in his mind, he really can't afford to do more than that, and here we have Wade trying to rest up so he can do more, and yet he's barely capable of doing anything," she muttered. "He should be in a hospital."

"There are no hospitals for people like our team," Tasha noted. "Sophia, you don't really understand all of this yet, so all I can do is ask you to have patience."

"I've got patience for Wade," she stated, "because really nobody else is in my life but him, and, as long as he cares, I'm willing to work through it. This is pretty mind-altering stuff, but I'm hanging on to the belief that he cares—but does he care enough?"

"Well, the fact that you're even here and that he didn't kick you out of his room"—Tasha smiled—"should let you know that he cares enough."

At that, Sophia glanced at her friend. "Would he have had enough power to veto my presence, given the circumstances?"

"If Wade didn't want you here, trust me. You wouldn't

be here," she noted. "And I can't really explain to you how that works. It's about protecting everybody, yes. But it's also about the team focusing on the bad guys—no distractions allowed, like petty fights among the team. Believe me. Terk would have read your intentions, as well as Wade's. If Terk found anything wonky, I just know that, on an energy level, he would have told you to basically *eff off*, and you wouldn't be here. Because, in your own mind, you would know without a doubt that this is the wrong place for you, and Terk would have read your mind to confirm that."

Sophia sat back and stared. "By that same token, then Wade *not* kicking me out of his bedroom ..."

Tasha laughed. "Maybe you should talk to Wade a little bit more about that. But I would take it as a very good sign."

Bolstered by that and yet still wondering how any and all of this worked, Sophia settled down.

Tasha added, "We need a physical location to go after this idiot who just broke into the computers."

"I know," Sophia agreed. "I was thinking that he had to be in another country because why would he be so foolish as to do anything close by, but still, for a good hacker, it's pretty easy to hide your tracks and to make it look like you're at a distance. If he's local though—as in, out of Europe, whether France and England—I would think he could then also be connected to the gunman who took out your admins or at least to the attack on the original team."

"And that's what I was thinking too. But the bad guys have cleaned up any of their gunmen—Peter, who was killed by Wade's own brother, who was killed by Coop, the man who kidnapped me, who was then killed by Wade and Terk."

Sophia gasped. "You were kidnapped? Wade's brother

was killed? Oh my God. I am missing so much information here."

Tasha laughed, waving a hand across her body. "It obviously all worked out for me. The trouble is … we need somebody alive to question."

"I don't know about *alive*," Sophia replied, "but at least something digital that we can grab on to for an identity." With that, the two of them went to work.

Not ten minutes later Tasha leaned back with a big sigh. "I may have found something. But it's not the Lui Pul name Wade gave us."

Sophia looked over at the picture on Tasha's screen. "I recognize him." Her tone was surprised, but she frowned. "Well, I think I do. I guess in a place like this, you must be careful what you say."

"No, not necessarily," Tasha stated. "If you have anything to offer, then please do. Otherwise we're all just spinning our wheels and wasting time."

"I met a guy named Randall Godwin, attending the same IT conference as me. And he looks like that." Sophia pointed to Tasha's screen.

"And why would he have been at your conference?" Tasha asked.

"For the same reason I was there. Looking at who was hiring and who wasn't, what was new in technology. I was checking the scenery. As in the Wade scenery." She sent a smirk in Tasha's direction.

"Right. Those were the days, weren't they? I miss the good old simple times." Tasha laughed. "I haven't done any of that shit in a very long time."

"I didn't plan on being there in the first place," Sophia noted. "But I was at loose ends, having switched out employers at the time. It was before I hooked up with Levi and Ice. Man, I wish I had hooked up with them earlier."

"They're good people," Tasha added.

"And apparently you found gold when you hooked up to this team," Sophia stated.

"I don't know. *Gold* is in the eye of the beholder, I guess. But, when your team gets wiped out, it is definitely not the word I would choose."

"Well, it just is such a typical shitty government move, and it makes you want to reach out and smack them."

"I'd like to reach out and kill them myself, but the one guy we suspected of being potentially either extremely gullible or directly involved—our contact, Bob, in the defense department—died in DC. I was using his log-in as a way to get into some government databases and had to change it when I realized he was no longer alive."

"Man, you guys are going through the bodies."

"Too many of them," Tasha murmured. "So this guy"— she nodded at the photo still on her screen, while she worked furiously on her keyboard—"he's got affiliations with Paris. His passport crossed into Belgium a couple days ago, but that doesn't mean he's still there. We need a location here for him," she murmured.

Sophia nodded. "Let me see what I can find. He was using Randall Godwin at the conference, but who knows if it's a fake name or not."

With that, the women ran a deep background check on this character.

Tasha was happy to have anything to do but was afraid to spend too much time focusing on this one guy and risk missing out on something else. "Hey, let's split up. You continue your search on Godwin, and I'll keep looking to see if I can come up with other possibilities for our primo hacker. I'm not getting anywhere on the guy Wade named. This Lui Pul."

"You do that," Sophia muttered, but she was already buried in the hunt. It took her twenty minutes before she let out a soft crow of success.

"What did you find?" Tasha asked.

"Bank accounts under Randall Godwin," she replied, with a note of satisfaction. "Everybody always does the first layer of encryption on bank accounts, but, once you start moving money, it leaves a trail, and I've found all kinds of those."

"What kind of money?"

"Millions," she stated succinctly.

"Well, that's even more enterprising then."

Between the two women, they hacked their way around, trying to uncover every single trail they could find.

"Sweet ... but this is just a tip of the iceberg," Sophia muttered. "We'll have to go deeper, as some of these accounts are bound to be fake."

And, with that, they kept digging, deeper and deeper.

"I'm not sure that we're still on the right track here," Tasha stated, "but at least now we have something to show the guys. We also have a Godwin address in the Liverpool area, although I found no sign that Randall has used it in a while. But it was under his father's name, and chances are, it's either a homestead family residence or it's something he uses as a front."

Sophia tapped her screen. "But dear old dad died over eighteen years ago."

"*Huh.* So how the hell do you keep it under a dead guy's name?"

"Lots of them in the family," Sophia explained. "Same last names, right? So, as far as the recordkeepers are concerned, nobody really gives a shit, as long as the bills are being paid."

"I think that's always the case. Pay your bills and stay under the radar and nobody cares. Except for people like us. And, for people like us, these guys are gold." Just behind Tasha, she heard a sound and turned to find Wade leaning against the doorjamb.

Sophia stood to assist him.

He lifted a hand. "I'm fine. Honestly, I'm fine."

She took a slow deep breath as she studied his face—still pale, huge circles under his eyes, obviously leaning against the doorframe for support. But a brightness in his gaze wasn't there before. "I know you don't want to be mothered," she admitted, "and I know you don't want that as part of any relationship, but it will take me a little time to not panic every time I see you looking like this."

He gave her a crooked smile. "You have a lot to get used to. It's one of the reasons I kept you out of this."

"Too late," she replied cheerfully. "I'm in, and I'm staying in."

He nodded. "I got that message, but some things you'll have to adjust to. Just like I've had to adjust to my *skills* too."

"And I will," she murmured. "Even if it takes me a while, I will. Don't write me off so quickly."

"Any chance of getting more food, or did Tasha eat it all?"

Tasha turned from the computer and glared at him.

He grinned back. "Nice to see some things haven't changed."

"Ha," she muttered. "At least you don't look like death

warmed over anymore."

"Oh, there may be a problem then"—he smiled—"because I sure feel like it."

"I'm sure you do." Tasha got up and walked over to help Sophia with Wade. "Bring him on over here, Soph, and we'll get some food into him."

"Hey, hey, hey, I'm not an invalid, so don't treat me like one."

"So stop acting like one," Tasha snapped back immediately.

He rolled his eyes at her. "Between the two of you …"

"You're thankful to be alive. Got it." Sophia gave him a big smile.

He laughed. "Well, there is that part too."

"And we're all grateful to have you alive," Tasha replied. "But the thing is, we have to keep you that way, so let's not have too many more arguments."

"Okay." He let Sophia lead him over to a seat at the kitchen table. Once he sat down and relaxed a little bit, it took the pressure off his legs and his spine. Yet, man, it looked like he couldn't stay upright for long. "I thought I was getting better, but this little bit of effort shows me that some weakness is definitely still here."

"Some," Sophia agreed. "Did you actually sleep? Or were you trying to work the whole time?" He just looked at her with a flat expression. She nodded. "You were working through it."

Tasha groaned. "Not sure how you think that'll help at all."

"It'll help," he stated, "because nobody else can do this."

"I get it. I do, but you also have to heal. Otherwise you can't help anyone, at all soon."

"I can do plenty," he stated in an insulted tone.

"Oh, please, enough with the ego." Tasha shook her head. "You know that you need to get a grip on that."

He glared at the two women. When he opened his mouth to snap back again, Sophia placed a bite of something in his mouth, stopping the onslaught of words. He continued to glare but chewed away furiously. By the time he was done with that, she popped another one in. "Fine." He raised his hand to block any more food. "Message received."

"Good. I highly suggest we ignore all of what was about to come out of your mouth. I can see that keeping you filled up periodically will make you a little easier to deal with." Sophia frowned. "Hungry people are no fun for anyone." She looked over the foodstuffs that Tasha has amassed and asked, "Are we saving this food for anything?"

"For us," Tasha stated, immediately coming over. "You want something?"

"I could use something," Sophia murmured.

"Help yourself. When this is gone, we'll get more."

"Sure, but getting more will also open ourselves up to problems, won't it?" Sophia asked.

"Not necessarily. We've done okay with that so far."

Sophia could sense the reticence in her friend's voice. "Maybe so, but every time we head out, it'll risk trouble."

"We still have to eat. We still have to maintain our reserves to keep going," Tasha stated. "So we can't just go without."

"Got it." At the moment there appeared to be lots of food, and no point in letting any of it go to waste either.

Tasha prepared a few sandwiches, and one arrived in front of Sophia. Once Tasha put a big one in front of Wade, Tasha sat down with her own.

As Sophia watched the two of them, something almost like an unspoken link was going on. "Can you guys talk in your heads?" Sophia asked suddenly.

Tasha looked at her in surprise. "I can't, not really, but he can."

"Really?" Sophia turned to Wade.

He shrugged. "Sometimes yes, sometimes no. However, since then, I've exhausted my reserve of energy, and my abilities got wiped out in the attack. So the answer now is *maybe*."

She smiled at the hint of sarcasm in his voice at the end. "Well, I'll take a maybe any day. I've heard inquiries about it happening, but I didn't know of any people directly who could do that."

"Inquiries from whom?" Tasha asked.

Looking at her friend, Sophia frowned. "Well, it was mentioned back at the conference, the same one Wade and I attended about a year ago. Some AI systems were circulating this info, how their software was supposedly enabling people to share telepathic communication."

"An AI system?" Wade stopped and stared at her. "Are you serious?"

She nodded and shrugged. "Yes, some implant."

He immediately sat back, crossed his arms. As Terk opened his bedroom door, Wade's gaze turned to his friend.

"Tell us more." Terk joined them at the kitchen table.

Sophia shrugged. "All I can tell you is the little bit I overheard from the conference, wandering around the vendors' booths, maybe at one of the separate speaker events, or even over dinner afterward." She turned to Wade. "You were there too."

He gave her a lopsided grin. "I was, but I didn't really

pay attention. I had other things on my mind."

She flushed at that. "Right. It was brought up during the conference somehow, but it seemed to be a futuristic suggestion, and I don't know how far into beta testing it was yet."

"But it's a possibility?" Tasha looked over at Wade. "In a way, it makes a whole lot more sense because we know of no sighting of any weapon like this before. Yet we've been monitoring weapons at this level for years."

Wade nodded slowly. "That's very true. We had absolutely no understanding of any of this prior to this psychic attack on our team. After Iran we thought we were the only gifted team. However, after our own attack on an energy level, now we're going on the assumption that somebody else had been building a team, whether of men like us or of maybe hardware or software to mimic what men like us can do."

"That is very possible." Terk nodded. "We have Wade, who can interact with technology on the ethers, so let's assume that others like him are out there. Now it seems that somebody else may be building a team using software, and that technology could be at the point where it is much easier to do so." He walked around the room, shaking his head. "We've always known that this software was a possibility and that it would happen at some point in time, but we hadn't figured it would happen this soon."

"Maybe that's our fault," Wade admitted. "When you think about it, an awful lot is out there that we are capable of doing that we haven't really been allowing ourselves to get into. We dropped the ball on the software angle, once we got so busy developing our own skills."

"Sure, but that's because we were developing natural

skills, existing skills," Terk explained. "I can't imagine doing that from scratch. Not with humans or IT."

Just then another door opened, and Damon walked through, slowly and carefully but mobile. Immediately Tasha got up and ran over. He opened his arms, and she gently snuggled in close. "Can't even do a stake-out without draining all my energy," Damon complained.

"Well, you did get shot recently," Tasha reminded him.

Sophia watched, her heart smiling, as she realized that her friend had, indeed, found a special relationship. "They look good together," she noted quietly to Wade.

At her side, Wade nodded. "They've been avoiding this relationship for a very long time. This chaos that we're in brought it all to a crunch."

"Good." Sophia nodded. "Sounds like us."

"Not quite," Wade argued. "I specifically walked away."

She turned and glared at him. "Yeah, and we'll have another discussion about that at some point."

He smiled. "Nope, not likely."

"We have to," she stated, "because I need to know that you'll be there for me, just like you need to know that I'll be there for you."

"I thought we already did that part." He frowned at her.

She nodded. "And we probably did. Maybe it's just my insecurity about you leaving again that is poking out its ugly head."

"Then you'll have to deal with that," he stated.

She laughed. "Just like that, *I'm* supposed to deal with it?"

"Yep, just like that." He grinned. "Although, with a little bit of time, I can help."

"I'm glad to hear that." She glanced at him, Wade tossing a wink her way. She smiled. "But there's still got to be other things in life."

"There's always other things in life," he noted. "However, right now, our focus isn't on relationships."

Motioning toward Damon and Tasha, who were walking toward them, Sophia added, "Sometimes good things in life happen for good people."

Quietly Wade added, "Believe me. They should have done this years ago. We've all been sharing the same office space, while they ignored each other."

"You mean, while he ignored her."

Wade looked at Sophia in surprise and then laughed. "How do you know?"

"Because Tasha wears her heart on her sleeve and always has," Sophia noted. "By and large, we're very much upfront and open people. It's just guys like you two who make things complicated."

A muffled snort came from a seat at the table.

Sophia looked over to find Terk grinning at her. "It's true," she stated.

"Oh, I know," Terk admitted. "I'm not arguing with you. You also have to understand the caliber of men you're working with. We deal with life-threatening situations all the time." He paused. "So bringing somebody in—somebody who we care about—automatically makes them a weapon to be used against you."

She nodded. "But sometimes I wonder if you might be better off sharing a short time with somebody great than a lifetime with nobody."

Terk studied her.

"And what do you know about that?" Wade asked stiffly.

"Only what I've learned while witnessing Merk and Levi's group," Sophia shared, "and I've learned more since I've come here, learned something special. I'd like to think we all want this shared experience of a true relationship over a lifetime of never having experienced one."

WADE STUDIED SOPHIA'S interactions with the group. She was fitting in better than he had expected. But then she didn't know the whole story about Terk's team, and Wade sure as hell wasn't up to telling her, at least not yet. She'd probably find out just enough to make her head for the hills, screaming. Every outsider thought they could handle this team's special skills, until it was turned their way. He looked over at Terk, sensing his boss's own perturbed emotions, and smiled. Terk was gearing up to head out.

"You're not coming," Terk told Wade.

"There's only you and Damon, and he's injured." Wade shrugged. "So I'm going."

"You are *both* recovering. And Merk is still in town, and I can tag along with him."

"Take him if you want," Wade agreed, "but I didn't think you wanted to be seen with your brother. Regardless I'm coming too."

"And your energy?" Terk asked in a mild tone.

Wade did a mental check. "It's not too bad," he replied cautiously.

At that, Terk raised his eyebrows. "*Not too bad* won't really cut it," he murmured.

"Well, let's say, it'll do better while we're outside than it will be in here."

"Meaning?"

"I'll just worry if I stay here," he noted.

"And everybody else will worry if you go," Terk argued.

"That's their problem."

Terk laughed. "Not quite, but some of this stuff comes right back down to you."

"Maybe, but we need to take action." Wade frowned. "We need answers, and we won't get them sitting here." He turned and asked Tasha and Sophia, "Did you find a location of our hacker?"

"We did," Tasha spoke up. He glanced over at her. "It's a residential address," she explained. "It looks like a family home. Not necessarily anybody is there, but this guy—the Randall Godwin that Sophia ran into at that conference— well, his dad, Randall Sr., died about eighteen years ago, and the home's still in his name."

"So it's potentially a location Randall's hoping nobody will expect him to be using personally."

"But wouldn't you think that they would?" Sophia asked. "Seems like it would be one of the first places you'd look."

"It is, and it isn't," Terk explained. "We assume that they expect us to find it, and maybe it's a trap. At the same time, we assume that it's a place too good for them to pass up using. So it's a chance, but one we have to take."

Sophia frowned at that but nodded. "I guess that makes some sense," she hedged, "but if they're using some special software—"

"I'm still stunned at that whole futuristic concept myself," Wade admitted, "but it would explain a lot."

Amusement immediately crossed Sophia's face. "You mean that there's nobody else quite like you guys?"

"There isn't anybody else quite like us," he stated, his

voice getting stronger. Then he glanced at her, grinned. "You just don't know all of it yet."

"Will I ever?" she asked.

He shrugged. "Depends on how you can handle what you do know." And, with that, he headed for the food, got himself a second sandwich because he needed the protein and the carbs. He looked over at Terk. "Are you sure you should be coming?"

"Not a whole lot of choice," he replied, "as you know very well."

Wade nodded. "That's the hell of it, isn't it?" He paused. "Who would have thought we'd be in this position right now?"

"No one, but it doesn't matter because we've got to deal with it regardless."

Wade nodded. "We need to do this." With that, he finished his sandwich and checked the weapons that they had available. While he was doing so, Terk was tanking up himself. Eating more than usual was good in a sense because the team would burn through the carbs, so they didn't have to find other sources for energy, if they ran low.

Sophia walked over to see if Wade needed anything.

He smiled at her. "I should be good." She frowned but didn't say anything. He knew she was worried—not a whole lot he could say. It still felt odd to have her here, yet it also felt … … right—as if all the time they were apart had never happened. But it had … …

She'd signed on to see all this through, and, whether she would make it through or not, he didn't know. He hoped so, but they had a lot ahead of them yet. He quickly slipped a handgun into his holster and checked that he had his knife in his belt.

DALE MAYER

She watched his movements with hooded eyes.

"I'll be fine."

"And if not, it's too damn bad anyway. Isn't it?" she muttered.

He nodded. "That's about the size of it."

She sighed. "I'll adjust."

"Good." He reached over, gave her a hard kiss, and then stepped back, as Terk joined them. "You ready?"

"Yeah," Terk replied. "Merk will meet us there."

"Is that the best answer?"

"Maybe not, but it's the one we've got."

CHAPTER 4

W ADE WATCHED AS Tasha seemed to check out him and Terk, as if checking each man's energy levels. "Don't worry, Tasha. Merk knows how shorthanded we are, so he may join us," Wade explained.

"I could come too," Sophia offered instantly.

Wade looked at her, smiling. "I know that you have field experience and that you're hell on wheels in so many areas, but honestly, we need you here. When things go ugly, it can get worse." He looked over at Damon and asked him, "You turned off your tracker?"

"Yeah, I did."

"Did it help?"

"It did at the time," Damon replied, standing up and walking toward them. "I just opened it, and then we had Tasha here shut it off internally."

"And?" Wade asked.

Damon looked over at Terk, who shook his head.

"So it should be okay," Wade stated. "Nobody knows or has our frequency."

"At least we're hoping nobody does," Terk corrected him. "If it comes to that, then, Tasha, you need to shut us down. Do you hear me?"

She immediately nodded. "I can do that," she confirmed. "I really don't want to though."

"We hear you, and we don't want it to be that way, but, if need be, that's our only option. It cuts down on the possibility of the bad guys tracking us."

"I get it," she noted.

And, with that, Terk and Wade headed out the back door. Taking alternative routes, they met at the vehicle several blocks away. Wade approached it quietly, searching it externally for any signatures or anything that was different. Then searched for anything that was wrong or shouldn't be there. It was hard to explain, but everything had a sense. Everything had an energy. Everything had something that leaves behind an impression or a mark or a spore or a signature of some kind, and that's what Wade was looking for. Seeing nothing, he hopped into the vehicle and turned it on.

Within seconds the passenger door opened, and Terk joined him. "Let's go," And they raced away into the night.

"ARE THEY WEARING trackers?" Sophia asked, almost in disbelief when they were gone.

Damon nodded. "Implants, yes. Something that we've always done in order to keep track of our guys' positions because of the work we do. It's not always a sure deal that we won't collapse or go down injured while on a job, so we don't want anybody to be picked up by the enemy, or we don't want a friendly fire situation either, should one of us be out of place," he noted. "The trackers have saved our asses more than a few times."

"Sure, but, Jesus, if I can hack into them, a lot of other people could too," Sophia noted.

"Well, that's something you get to work on right now."
Then Damon added, "Tasha will make sure that it's not
trackable. We had some problems with mine, so we just
turned it off," he muttered. "But, Sophia, if you can find a
way to make sure nobody else could access it or use it, that
would be an awesome upgrade. We need to know where our
guys are in order to keep them safe."

"And how can you keep them safe?" she asked, studying
him. "It's not like you're in any shape to do much."

"I will do what's needed," he replied, his voice hard.
"Don't ever assume otherwise." With that, he turned and
headed back to the bedroom.

"Oops." Sophia turned to Tasha. "I think I've upset
him."

"They're men," Tasha replied, with a casual wave of her
hand. "You have to realize that, with their capabilities
impaired, they're supersensitive to the suggestion that they
might be lesser beings."

"God, how can they be less?" Sophia asked in shock.
"These guys are machines."

"Not quite. They get hurt, and they bleed just like the
rest of us," she noted. "But they're always very touchy. Right
now particularly because of the attack on everyone and the
knowledge that we still have a good share of our team in
danger of not recovering. They all feel like they should have
done more."

"Could they have done more?"

"Not unless they had some intel as to what was going
on," Tasha replied. "The attack was completely out of the
blue. Our program was discontinued, and we had just shut
down the field office. I was taking a few days off. I'm not
even sure what all of them were doing. I was going home to

lick my wounds." She paused. "After all those years of loving that idiot"—she sighed—"and suddenly, just like that, the gig was over, and I'd probably never see him again. But instead we were attacked that night."

"And the team thinks the US government was involved?"

"It could be the Iranian government. It could be any other government who has reasons to be upset with us. We don't want to draw too many conclusions and lock it down to just one suspect, afraid that we are potentially overlooking other answers, and, by making that assumption, they'll risk making a mistake in shutting down other leads."

"I know it can be hard when things get tough and you narrow your focus too much," Sophia replied, "but still you have to make some assumptions in order to find any pathway forward."

"Well, you focus on making the trackers untraceable by others," Tasha stated, "and I'll go hunting." With a cup of hot coffee in her hand, Tasha went back to her computer.

Sophia looked at the food and realized that she had barely sat down for a moment to grab anything herself except for the sandwich earlier. She ate another one, then picked up a cup of coffee and headed to her station. If Wade would be out there and had a subcutaneous tracker, she wanted to make sure no way in hell anybody would find him but her. After twenty minutes, she realized that would be easier said than done. "I can see them," she noted, "but I can't find a way to track them other than through the system that we have, which would suggest anybody accessing their trackers were hacking into our system."

"And having just kicked them all out, it should take them some time before they get access again." Tasha was at her side, working furiously on the keyboard.

Yet Sophia felt like she didn't have anything to contribute. That thought just pissed her off. She really wanted to find a way to further protect these guys. She went back to keeping an eye on the movements of the two men, and then brought them up on a satellite, compliments of Stone through Levi.

"You're really worried about them?" Tasha asked her.

"I feel like I lost him long enough," Sophia admitted.

"Did he really just walk out on you?"

"Yep. Well, we were at the same conference as our suspected hacker, Randall Godwin, and Wade stood me up for dinner, then never called or anything. Apparently after that, he was attacked on another job. So about a year ago he got injured and realized how dangerous it was to have anybody in his life, which finalized his decision to keep me out."

"Ah, that sounds familiar," Tasha replied. "They all do that. It's frustrating as hell. In my case, Damon wouldn't even come close to me for all the years that I worked with him. And that drove me bonkers. I knew something was between us, but he wasn't having anything to do with it. I couldn't find a way to break the impasse and just assumed he didn't like me."

Tasha shook her head. "It took the attack and him thinking I'd been killed for him to realize that life is too short, and, if I were willing, then he wouldn't turn down the opportunity to live a fuller life. Apparently he really cared and had been denying himself all that time as well."

"Men are such idiots," Sophia muttered under her breath.

"I heard that," Damon said from the doorway.

Tasha shrugged. "Don't care if you did or not," she

snapped. "You're an idiot." Tasha openly grinned.

"I was trying to protect someone I'd been so in love with all that time," Damon admitted, unsuccessfully trying not to sound defensive.

"Yeah, and, at the same time, you were cheating Tasha of living her life to the fullest." Sophia shook her head.

Damon shrugged. "We'll never agree on that, just as I doubt Tasha will agree with me on why I did what I did," he replied. "But I never doubted that it was the right thing." And, with that, he turned and walked back into his room again.

"Wow, these guys all just walk around like they're made of clouds, don't they?" Sophia asked.

Tasha burst out laughing. "Yep."

Sophia added, "It seems like every time I speak, somebody walks out of the room. That bugs the hell out of me."

"But what you have to realize is that absolutely nothing will be hidden from these guys. Or us either. We may not have their special skills, but we've got our gut intuition, and we're right here, always in observation mode. So, in a way, that's a good thing because then you don't have everybody wondering what's going on behind their backs. It's all very open and honest here."

"Well, a lot could be said for that," Sophia admitted. "It's just weird in a way, to be so exposed. I mean, Terk can read minds, after all."

"Well, get used to it because this is the kingdom of weird," Tasha stated, "and there's really nothing to be done but deal with it or walk."

"Well, I'm not walking," Sophia snapped.

"Good!" Tasha replied. "Get angry, but find a way to keep our guys safe. Particularly if you want to pursue that happy-ever-after."

"Do you think there will be something like that for me and Wade?"

"I would like to think so," Tasha agreed. "But again, you have to convince these guys that we're safer with them than without them, and that's not the easiest argument to win."

"No, they're all stubborn, aren't they?" And, with that, Sophia returned to studying the software. As she watched, she saw something funky going on. "Shit." Sophia straightened up, tapped the monitor. "I presume this is your software added here."

"Correct. Well, it's largely mine. I piggybacked it on another program. Why?"

Sophia took a look at it. "Somebody is already trying to get in."

Tasha took a quick look. "Dammit. I'm afraid they're already in." The two women immediately started working to find the intruder. "Do you know what they're after?" Tasha asked Sophia.

"By the looks of it, they're after the tracking."

"Kill it," Tasha stated in a hard voice. "Immediately."

"No, we can't kill our trackers. We'll never keep track of Wade and Terk," Sophia argued. "I'm not doing that."

"You got a better idea?"

"Yeah, I do," Sophia noted. "Let's catch these motherfuckers." And, with that, she went to work.

WADE HEARD THE text message *beep*, and, as soon as he opened Tasha's text, he told Terk, "Tasha says somebody's in the system, and they are targeting the trackers."

"Do you want to disable them?" Terk asked.

"I asked how bad it was, but she just said that Sophia is working on it."

"Well, if Sophia is working on it, presumably they are in charge, and the decision is theirs. Tell them to shut it down if there are no other options. I was really hoping the tracking would work unobstructed from now on. Otherwise we're more than blind. I just don't want anybody coming to our headquarters. The women are pretty well on their own."

"Not quite," Wade replied. "Damon is there."

"Sure. But we also know what can happen when we're shorthanded. Let me check in on them." With that, Terk shifted slightly and closed his eyes.

A weird buzz of energy followed. Wade really was hopeful that Terk would get ahold of Damon, so he could be on extra alert and keep Tasha and Sophia safe, if anything should happen at their new headquarters. Besides, they needed to keep a low profile, since the last thing they wanted was to tip off the wrong people that Terk's team had a new base. Were there enough safeguards in place in case someone showed up? "What if they're using that new software? What if they are using it against us?" Wade asked Terk.

"How so?"

"Well, what if they were using it on our trackers?"

"I don't think they could have inserted any hardware into our computer system without us knowing." And then he stopped and sent a questioning look to Wade.

At that, Wade shook his head. "Not any software either. I would know from my latest computer fix."

"I know that you *think* you would know," Terk replied, gauging Wade's response carefully.

"But I'm sure. I don't think they ever got a hold of me."

"I'll go ahead and say this. I really do get it, and I'm sorry because I'm not trying to piss you off. But we have to consider all the alternatives, and, right now, that one is starting to look like a possibility."

"Well, who's to say that?" Wade asked. "Any software would have to be compatible with my mind, and is there even a system as advanced as the human mind yet?"

"Just because we don't know about something doesn't mean it doesn't exist," Terk argued. "More likely," he added, "they've probably connected via software, hacking right into our trackers. Maybe the attack is originating from our trackers."

Wade shook his head. "I like the sound of the second option over hacking our brains. Right about now, I'm feeling a little sensitive about anybody hacking into anything that's ours."

Terk laughed bitterly. "Especially our brains."

"I don't want to imagine it, but that is my job," Wade replied. "We've got enough chaos and nightmares going on in our scenarios without having to worry about someone hacking into the most private part of us. When chaos happens, you know that it'll happen in a bad way."

"There's always something new or different happening in our field," Terk stated.

Wade shook his head as he approached a corner, before driving around it. "Always some new shit show and we must be one step ahead of the game."

"So, in this instance," Terk muttered, "by the time we're done with whoever's been attacking us and now tracking us, we have to make sure that whatever software they have is completely gone. We need to destroy it entirely, or else nobody in the world will be safe."

CHAPTER 5

"OKAY, I'VE GOT our interloper isolated," Sophia muttered to herself. "Now let's wrap this guy up and tag him and see if we can track him backward," she muttered. At her side, she felt Tasha watching her every move.

"That's good that you got him," she noted in admiration. "That will make a huge difference."

"Will it? It'll only make a difference if he doesn't know what I'm doing and if we can keep him separated from getting where he wants to go."

"And I get that." Tasha watched as her friend worked for a bit, then headed back over to her own tasks.

The fact that Tasha was leaving Sophia to do this was a huge vote of confidence. But then it was rare for her to actually require any oversight when it came to this stuff. She took pride in her work, and it was the work that she loved to do. It's just that it didn't always work out the way that she wanted it to. But then what else was new? Sometimes life just sucked.

Like when Wade had walked away from her. Sophia had thought for sure she'd found something absolutely amazing; then, just like that, it was gone. It had been a hard lesson, and even now was something that she wasn't sure she was completely ready to forgive him for. Understanding was one thing, but allowing it to happen again was another. And while that was a completely different issue, she also knew that she would take any chance she could to keep him in her life because he was worth it.

Which also made her vulnerable.

She stared at the screen in front of her. "No fucking way, asshole." The interloper's code was sliding sideways, looking for another door. She immediately placed more blocks.

"Are you playing with him?" Tasha asked.

"I'd like to blast him to smithereens," she snapped, "but I don't really understand what he's after, so I thought it was more valuable to figure that out, instead of just wiping him out. I'm also trying to color-code every step that he makes so, when he retreats, we can follow him. Plus, follow what he did later."

"I like the sound of that," Tasha admitted. "Just make sure that you don't play with him to the extent that everything else gets lost."

"No, I won't," she stated. "Too much at stake here."

"That is very true," Tasha agreed, with a smile. "It's really nice to have you on board."

"Why? Because you're not alone?" Sophia asked, with a gentle laugh.

"To a certain extent, yes," Tasha admitted. "Losing Mera has been really tough. We were friends and had worked together the last couple of years. We hadn't made any plans after the team was disbanded, as both of us were trying to figure out what we wanted to do next. But, damn, when you lose someone and when you realize that you didn't even have a chance to reconnect, it just pisses you off."

"I can see that," Sophia muttered, as she worked away on her screen. She didn't dare give this guy an inch without making sure that she knew exactly where he was traveling, but he was also being way too cagey, and that worried her. "This guy is really good," she muttered.

"Have you considered that it could be a bot?"

She stopped and looked over at her friend. "Jesus, no, I didn't."

"Well, I think that may be what you've got going on here," Tasha stated. "From the looks of it, it seems way too quick."

"Not necessarily," Sophia argued. "You know that you and I would be just as fast."

At that, Tasha laughed. "You've got a point there." She looked at the screen. "Look. He's starting to do a run again."

And, with that, Sophia headed back over and blocked every corner he tried. She added a bit more code to trace the steps, and then she finally said, "Okay, I think he's good to go."

"And what does that mean?" Damon asked from behind her.

"Just that I think he's good to leave, and we can track him back as he goes." With that, her screen started to do a weird spin.

Damon gasped. "What the hell is that?"

"Exactly what I want," Sophia replied reassuringly. "He'll have to retreat now." Even as they watched, a weird red light went through the screen. "That's my work right there"—she pointed—"tracking him back." As she leaned back in her chair, she added, "I put in checkpoints." She continued to stare at her screen.

"Well, he bounced out of Lisbon." She waited. "And then back out of Iran." She shook her head. "He's not done. And now we've got a signal bouncing out of New York."

Tasha smiled. "He's trying to hide his tracks, but he's

got a tail, and he doesn't know how to get rid of it."

"So the problem with that now," Sophia noted in a conversational tone, "is that he doesn't dare go home, at least not immediately. Because, when he goes home, I'll know where home is for him."

"But still, you'll only get a country, won't you?" Damon asked.

"Nope," she stated. "I'll get his goddamn computer." They all sat waiting tensely, as the retreat went on. "He went back through Lisbon again," she noted. She glanced over to see that even Tasha had stopped and was watching. "We just have to make sure we don't lose him at this point."

"I know, right?" Tasha stated. "But I can't even begin to get on to him while you're there."

"I know. Let me just keep handling this," Sophia muttered. "He'll have to go home eventually."

"But it might take him a while," Tasha replied. "Only when he believes he's shaken you off."

"And yet this isn't about time now," Sophia noted. "No matter where he goes or when, my tracer on him will follow and will keep up over the hours." She got up, stretched. "Are you guys okay if I go lie down for a bit?"

Tasha nodded right away. Damon opened his mouth and then closed it, looking over at Sophia.

Sophia just nodded. "Okay, I'll go grab ten then." And she walked over to her bed, then laid down and crashed.

In the distance, Sophia heard Damon ask Tasha, "Was that wise to just leave all this open?"

"It's not open. Like she said, her tracer is running, so I can handle it from here. She needs sleep, and she didn't get any," she reminded him.

"I know. It just seems odd that now that we've got

somebody on the run that she gets up and walks."

"She's not walking. She's planning ahead. There'll be a lot of work to do as soon as we find out where the hacker is, so right now is her only chance to grab a break." Tasha smiled. "It's actually really smart because, after this, we'll be working our asses off, running down whoever these assholes are."

"Do you think we'll catch something out of this?" Damon asked, sounding skeptical.

"I do think so," Tasha agreed. "Yes," she added a bit more firmly.

Sophia curled up on the side of the bed, pulled a blanket lightly over her and closed her eyes. She could still hear the murmured whispers, but it didn't matter what the whispers were. Tasha was correct. Whatever the hell was happening would happen as soon as the intruder landed at home. So Sophia needed to be awake and alert for that. For now, she needed to sleep.

WADE STUDIED THE outside of the Godwin family residence. "It looks like a huge old aristocratic estate, big money here. Well, there *was* big money anyway," he stated, "but you can see things haven't been maintained. The gates are looking ever-so-slightly tilted to the side, so whoever had the money doesn't necessarily have it anymore or just doesn't care enough. Or maybe they let it look this way on purpose, just to throw everybody off, to make it look abandoned."

"That's a possibility too," Terk agreed. They were waiting in their vehicle for Merk to show. When Terk suddenly opened the truck's passenger door, Wade looked over at him.

"What?" Terk asked, coming around to Wade's side of the truck.

"Have you always been able to talk to your brother like that?"

"Most of the time. It made growing up a lot easier."

"You think?" Wade shook his head.

"Now, if everyone around us knew, I'm sure it would have driven them nuts."

"Probably, but, like most kids, we didn't really care about anyone else. It was cool to us."

"And Merk can talk to you that way?"

"Sometimes. Much less so now. It's like he grew out of it, and I grew into it."

"Interesting phrase."

"I don't think he cared about it as much, whereas for me it was everything."

"So maybe he didn't want it, and you just accepted it openly."

"That's possible. I never really looked at it that way. Not the easiest growing up like this," Terk muttered. "Wasn't any room for people like me out there."

"Well, there is now," Wade noted. "Only because you made room for it. You made room for all of us, and, for that, we're damn grateful."

"I don't know," Terk stated. "You probably would have been just fine doing what you were doing before I found you."

They slipped across the road toward the front gate. Even as he thought about those words, Wade knew Terk was wrong. "You're wrong, you know?" he stated, when they reached the other side. "I wasn't doing anywhere near as well as I am now."

"And that's because every time we ignore our abilities, it's fine for a little while, but eventually it catches up to you. You think you're doing great, and you do your best to be happy, but how can you really be happy when only half of you is functioning on the inside?"

"Well, you convinced us of the right way obviously, since we became a team, doing the job," he stated. "But you know that it hasn't been the easiest journey."

"No, it's never been easy," Terk replied. "All we can do now is hope that, when this is over, we can get back to living our lives."

"And then what? Have you thought about that?"

"I have actually, but I can't really say anything about it until I figure out where I'm at. Only having two of my team here, we better focus on the here and now."

"Jesus," he said, "don't say that."

"And yet it's hard for me to think of anything else," he replied. "We have a lot of really good men who are down right now."

"Anybody else starting to surface?"

"Yeah, Gage is doing better," Terk noted.

"Well, that would be a hell of a thing because he could be looking into this location right now to see if anybody was here."

"And I've talked to him," Terk added.

"Jesus … have you?" Wade stopped and looked over at Terk, with joy on his face. "Is he well enough to talk? When this is over, I'll go see him."

"Yeah … well, I've been talking to him the other way," he replied a bit evasively.

"Ah, now that makes more sense, but, if he can even communicate that well," Wade added, "then we've got improvement happening."

"Definitely improvement, just not enough," Terk noted, with a gentle smile. "I'm trying to feed him energy to heal because he's not strong enough to reach out and take it."

"That's dangerous, Terk. For you." Wade looked at him. "You know that."

"It's not dangerous because the world around us is full of energy."

"Don't give me that shit. You know it's dangerous because you're likely to wear yourself down, and Gage won't have control yet. He'll be pulling and taking what he needs, without worrying about your needs."

"Of course," Terk agreed. "Right now he's still unconscious, but he's pulling, and he's asking for the energy, and I'm sending it."

"Of course you are. Shit." Wade groaned. "I would have offered, but I'm not healthy enough to be of any use."

"Nope, you're not, which is why I'm doing it," Terk murmured. "So don't get pissy about it. Gage will be a little bit longer but don't be surprised if he reaches out soon to talk."

"I'd be more than happy to talk to him," Wade offered. "Jesus, that's the best news I've heard in a long time," he muttered. "Thanks for that." And they headed toward the house. "You think we should just approach from the front?"

"Merk is doing reconnaissance, so we'll wait for him to reach out." So far they didn't see any sign of life.

"Well, it'd be nice if nobody is home," Wade noted.

"On the other hand, it'd be nicer still if somebody is here."

"That's just because you're eager to question somebody, anybody, to get some answers," Wade replied. "I don't think the answers will be quite so quick to come by."

"They never are," Terk agreed. "But we can always hope that maybe, one of these days, somebody will give us something helpful."

Wade laughed. With that, they approached the front gate only to find that it wasn't even closed. And it opened soundlessly. "That's the first sign," he stated, "that maybe we're in the right place."

Terk nodded, understanding that, when gates were soundless, it often meant that people liked to slip in and out without letting everybody in the neighborhood know where they were. It also meant that others could slip in and out as well.

"Cameras?" Wade asked.

"Merk says he's not seeing anything, though he finds that very suspicious."

"You think?" Wade replied. "Either it's completely innocent or it's 100 percent suspicious. There's no in-between when it comes to this shit." And, without further discussion, they headed around the side of the house, keeping low, hiding behind the bushes as they could.

When they got up to the side of the house, Wade heard an odd sound. Stepping back out of sight, he saw Terk and Merk approach each other, not a word spoken between them, but sharing a half smile as they kept on going. Wade followed Terk and Merk as they headed to the rear of the house.

"Talk about being threats in the night that nobody saw," he murmured to himself. But these two were something else again. And they were damn good at it. Wade could only hope to ever be half as good. He knew that Merk didn't have a whole lot to do with these special skills. But shit, for a guy who didn't have those extra skills, he was pretty damn capable in the middle of nowhere. As they approached the back of the house, Wade looked around. "I'm not seeing any sign of life."

"No, neither are we. Let's go in."

The door was locked but had it been anything other than that, it would have made Wade feel like they had an open invitation to a trap. He quickly picked the lock, then stepped inside and looked around. A high-end kitchen was the first surprise. The old estate had been modernized somewhere along the line in the last decade. So why was nobody here?

As they moved through the kitchen to the living room, they searched the complete main floor, then the three of them moved through the rest of the house. As Wade reached the master bedroom, he pushed open the door, then slipped inside and froze. Making a mental call out to Terk, he sent, *You need to come here.*

Terk immediately came in his direction, Merk on his heels, looking around carefully. They stepped into the master bedroom with Wade and winced. Whoever had been living on the property was likely to be the guy lying here with a bullet in his head and his body twisted at an odd angle. His whole bed had been covered with a heavy translucent plastic sheet, taped to the bedframe securely, hiding the smell. Time of death? In the last few days probably.

"Well, that explains some things," Terk stated. "Now we need to figure out what they've been using the house for."

Wade studied the layout of the body and realized no way this was a suicide. It was definitely a murder, and, if that were the case, then they were right. "Somebody wanted the property. But was this guy an accomplice or a victim? Is he related to the owner?"

Wade stopped, looked at the body again, then took a photo and sent it to Tasha with a text message. **Track this guy for us.** When his phone vibrated not too much later, while they were searching the basement, he pulled it out and checked it.

"Tasha says it's the same Godwin family. Youngest son, Rodney. Had been married, two kids. The divorced mom and his kids live in Belgium now." He opened a second message. "Apparently the hacker trying to get to our trackers has returned home, and he is in Liverpool. They have another address for us to check out." The two brothers looked at him and nodded. "We need to get this place searched, then get to the other location."

"I'll go do a reconnaissance on the other one," Merk stated. "Give me the address. I'll be in touch in two hours." In a moment the second Liverpool address was quickly passed to him, and he was gone.

Wade looked over at Terk. "Let's take another look around." At Terk's raised eyebrow, Wade added, "I feel like I'm looking at some secret base here or something. I'm not sure what we're looking at, but it could be just as simple as the bad guys needed a place to secret away and used this house as a front that nobody can connect them to. Or the Godwin family are the bad guys." Just then his phone beeped again. "It's Sophia. Ah, shit."

He turned to Terk. "Our co-owner here, Rodney, was a software developer for NSA for ten years, and then he went off on his own, establishing a private company. Doing something special. No idea what that was. The company name is registered under his own."

"So, he worked as a contractor," Terk noted. "It's much

easier to keep things contained."

Wade gave her the go-ahead to look into the company and to unearth what this guy was up to and where it might lead. "Sophia is on it. Those two are good."

"I know." Terk grinned. "Even if these new relationships do cause some distractions among us all."

"Maybe, but we're working through that," Wade replied. "You were still right to bring in Sophia. She's damn good."

"I know that, and I've heard it from several other people. I've considered her over the years, the last year in particular, but it was never the right time."

"Yeah, well, how about now?" he asked, looking over at his boss, with a sheepish grin. "If she's not here full-time and permanent, then she's really not here."

"She'll get that figured out pretty damn fast," Terk stated. "Don't you worry. I didn't bring her in lightly, and I did a full check, as much as I could. Her whole focus has been to find out what the hell happened to you." He smiled.

"Great, so you knew that and brought her here?" he asked. "Why would you do that?"

"She likes you, and her rage isn't really rage."

"Then what is it?" He couldn't believe that she'd been hanging on to that all this time.

"It came from her heart, Wade. It came from love," Terk told him, "and no way I could let that go unresolved, not when I saw the same conflict within you."

CHAPTER 6

S OPHIA WAS BUILDING a program to try to keep the men
safe. She wanted to track not only when other people
approached their team but whenever the team's heart rates
increased. Her phone rang, and, once she glanced at it, she
saw it was Wade. "What's up?"

"This dead guy here, we have a laptop."

"Open it and turn it on," As soon as he did that, she
asked, "Wade, can you find an IP address? I want to log in to
this thing remotely." It didn't take him long, and then she
was inside. "Okay," she replied, "leave it to me, and I'll see
what's there and copy the data, then strip it. When the cops
come, they'll grab that for sure."

"Yeah, they will. Okay, over and out."

She laughed at that funny send-off and turned to look at
Tasha. "We've got a laptop."

"Good," she muttered. "Let's see what the hell this guy
has got in there." It didn't take them long. He might have
been a developer, but he wasn't thinking security in terms of
Fort Knox–type encryption. "I guess he'd come home and
work a bit and then write down ideas and sometimes log into
work."

Not much here they could gather. But they knew better.
Beneath the surface was always something. And, of course,
that was the downfall for everybody because, the minute you

keystroke in, somebody else could keystroke in behind you, following your pathway. And that's what Tasha and Sophia were doing.

"Okay, we have the company account, and we have his personal emails, and we also have the banking." Tasha immediately clicked on that because money was just plain interesting for everyone. Not everyone knew how to handle money or how to hide it, and, if this guy didn't think he was doing anything illegal, there was a good chance that he hadn't been trying to hide anything either. "Well, for a software developer, he's doing just fine," Tasha noted beside her.

Sophia winced. "Good point. Do you think they silenced him?"

"Hell yeah, I think they silenced him," Tasha stated bluntly. "The same way as they will silence everybody in their pathway."

"Nice guys." Sophia continued to peruse the data. "Well, he's got a couple million stacked up, and he's been searching for flights to Jamaica," she reported, "while looking into financial institutions in the Canary Islands. The trouble with that is," she noted, "he'd need a broker."

"Well, he could have gotten one pretty damn fast if they'd given him a chance."

"He was a developer, not a hacker, and this makes it very clear."

"Right," Tasha nodded. "The problem with that is, even though he wasn't a hacker, he was working on this 'special project,' which has led him into dark and ugly waters, even though he apparently didn't know it," Tasha noted sadly. "He was set up right from the beginning."

"And it's not the first time we've seen that," Sophia muttered. "Too often the brilliant ones are brilliant because they're good at what they do, but they're also fairly focused and narrow-minded, not necessarily worrying about everything else. But still, security has got to be accounted for."

"Sure, but has he got anything more than the basics?"

"Yeah, he does, so there you go. He probably thought nothing of it because he was working on his own stuff for his own company. He probably was thinking more along the line of IT theft, not having somebody kill him. Or having to hide his tracks."

"That's a good point," Tasha remarked.

By the time they were done, they had his bank accounts and all the statements as far back as they could go, and every assessment possible in terms of what he was doing or what he thought he was doing, including the company documents and even his developer model.

"He was working on software for tracking," Sophia noted, "and communications hooking to the eardrum using special vibrations."

"Jesus," Tasha replied, "so it's something that they could wear as a start then possibly implant."

"He was pretty excited about it, from his notes. It seems like they didn't give him a whole lot of rest. He has been at it for a while."

"Or he was being pushed, and, for all we know, he was being threatened."

"And that's something that we'll get to in a little bit," Sophia noted, "because, if it's here, it should be in the emails."

"Good point." Tasha looked over at her. "First, let's see if we can grab a cell phone. Or at the very least a number."

"Great idea," Sophia replied. After a few moments she

called out to Tasha, "I have a phone number." After giving her the number, she asked, "Do you think that'll help?"

"Sure it will," Tasha muttered. "Especially if I can get a history of his calls."

And, with that, after a few moments Sophia printed off his phone calls for the last year. With a hard copy in place, she turned back to the digital file and sorted, looking for repeat numbers, anything that was common, and trying to determine how many individual numbers there were, then determining what they were. Three were take-out places on the readout, which she thought was great.

In her experience most developers tended to get hooked into their work, and they rarely thought about eating. When they did, it was more of an afterthought and about fueling the brain, and he was just proving her right by being a creature of habit. "Okay, so we've got this guy who's seriously working on something pretty damn exciting. He can see the value, but he doesn't see the pitfalls ahead."

"Or maybe he didn't think that the pitfalls would apply to him," Tasha suggested.

Sophia winced at that. "That's happened way too many times, hasn't it?"

"All the time, if you think about it. They think they've got something that's golden and think the rest of the world'll play fair. The rest of the world is just waiting for them to come up with something that they can step in and take. It's not even so much about paying for it. That's got nothing to do with it really. It's about making sure that nobody even knows that this kind of software is available. This guy didn't stand a chance, right from the moment he started having success in his development."

"So, the better question is, who approached him? Because that person is the one who led him down the wrong path."

They turned their attention to checking it out. "Okay, so we've got five numbers he called the most." Sophia handed them off to Tasha. "Let's run them and see who's on the other end."

When she came back a few minutes later, Tasha stated, "We've got three names and two unregistered."

"Burner phones," Sophia noted, with a nod. "Got it. Now this is getting interesting. I mean, this guy has come up with something great and …"

Tasha added, "Gets approached by somebody who knew exactly what to do with that information."

"Bingo," Sophia said a moment later, when she got into the emails. "He reached out to two people online. He used a code word, so he was being smart, but blows it by saying he had developed some new software for intelligence operations."

"Well, that'll just trigger all kinds of searches, from the wrong kinds of people," Tasha stated.

"Those people out there," Sophia stated in disgust, "they just trawl the internet, looking for this stuff. Then they log in, check it out, and get even closer to find out who the hell is talking."

"It may not have been these people at all."

"Maybe not, but somehow somebody found him interesting," she muttered, as just she kept going through it. "Okay, I'm doing an analysis on all this. We'll print up a bunch of hard copies, and then we'll do a summary and send it to the guys."

"Well, they'll be back soon enough, so let's make sure we have something to show for it," Tasha noted. "The paperwork will happen down the road. This is definitely an on-the-fly moment. Merk has gone off to the second address that we gave them."

Sophia looked up and frowned. "I'm used to things going a little bit slower," she noted cautiously. "But I guess it's all about being quick and adaptable."

"Exactly, and, in this case, quick and adaptable means able to spin on a dime."

With that, Sophia grinned. "Not a problem." She started isolating the information. "I guess we don't want to start spamming the team with texts, do we?"

"Nope, we don't. I wonder if this is the same old story?"

Sophia looked over at her friend. "Meaning?"

"Software guy pokes his head up and says, 'Hey, I've got something fantastic. Who wants to pay for it?' And then he lines up visits from multiple people, who say they're interested. One of them gets there ahead of time, without making an appointment—or poses as one of the others or something. The details don't matter, but the important part is, he kills our developer, takes the information, and runs."

"Yet they didn't take his laptop," Sophia reminded her. "We'll have to ask the guys where the laptop was because either that's a setup or they were interrupted. Or they expected to come back and didn't find it."

"Or," Tasha added, "they did exactly what we're doing and made a copy of everything on there."

At that, Sophia frowned. "That wouldn't be good," she muttered.

"No, but look at the bright side. What we're doing and why we're doing it. It's as simple as that."

Sophia nodded. "I get it. Don't worry. It just means we're late to the party."

"The guy is dead. That means we're already late to the party," Tasha reminded her. With that, the two women went back to work.

When Sophia's phone rang the next time, she answered it. "I have information if you want it."

"I want it," Wade stated, and she quickly relayed what they'd found.

"And he already has millions in recent transactions, but not in the last thirty days," she added. "So I think he was still potentially looking for a buyer."

"But that also means that he wasn't necessarily—" Then he stopped. "Hang on a minute. I thought he had a contract with another company."

"Maybe, but maybe he realized what he had and decided to branch out a little," she replied caustically. "Maybe the dollar figures made more sense to him if he opened it up to other people."

"All he did was open himself up to getting shot," Wade stated.

"You know what? I'm not sure this guy really thought that far ahead. I think he thought that he was the one in the driver's seat and would ensure he got a little more out of this deal than he originally planned."

"Right," Wade noted. "That other address … we haven't heard back from Merk yet."

"Okay," she replied, "I'll get a satellite on it."

"Let me know if you see Merk approaching."

"Got it." Sophia hung up but texted him back. **Where did you find the laptop?**

Bedroom, on the bedside table.

"Damn." Sophia looked over at Tasha. "The laptop was on the bedside table, right there, open for anybody to find."

Tasha nodded. "Which means they probably just took everything off it. Could also mean the camera was on, and someone was watching. And that also means there could be a second computer."

Sophia grabbed her phone, called Wade. "You could be on camera, with the laptop connected to a second computer."

Wade laughed. "Way ahead of you, honey." Then he hung up again.

Sophia shook her head. "Are they always ten steps ahead of you—or is that just me?"

"Don't worry about it. Better to say it twice than to not have it considered in the first place."

"I guess so." Sophia nodded.

"But we won't know at this point, not from our vantage point anyway, so we can't worry about it." Tasha shrugged. "The guys will always have more intel for us. And we'll share ours with them as we uncover it."

"Gotta stop the worrying. I hear you, but again it's really frigging irritating when we're last to the party."

Tasha laughed. "Well, let's make sure we're first to the next one."

"Speaking of which, Wade wants a satellite check on Merk at the new address," Sophia relayed.

Tasha immediately nodded. "I have it up already."

"You're good." Sophia laughed.

"Well, I've been working with these guys for a while, and I know they need everything done fast. The minute you get an address, it's best to just pull all the related information you can."

"Got it."

As Sophia checked back on her own software, Tasha

looked over at her friend's screen and asked, "So, what is that?"

"I'm checking on the team," Sophia stated. "I was trying to build a program that would let us know when the team was in trouble. Giving us their location, heartbeat, and checking for data in the vicinity."

"Well, they probably wouldn't appreciate it." Tasha stared in fascination at Merk's data that had popped up on the screen. "I mean, I approve because I don't want to see anybody hurt, but I guarantee you that the guys will get upset."

Surprised, Sophia turned toward Tasha and frowned. "Why would they be upset?"

Damon answered the question, as he slowly walked toward them. "Because we have unusual methods and energy needs. When we get low, we need to recharge, so the information that you're pulling up will sometimes be personal and private. No one likes to be laid bare, you know?"

She stared at him in surprise. "Seriously? How the hell did vital statistics become so complicated?"

"Because the team can raise and lower them at will," he replied. "Again, it's back to the fact that you just don't have the same knowledge of the team yet."

She shook her head. "Good God, it makes me wonder if I ever will."

"You will," he noted cheerfully. "It'll just take a little bit of time."

She nodded, then looked over at Tasha. "Maybe I'll just run everything through you for a while."

Tasha laughed. "You're doing just fine, and you're not wasting time, by the way, because this is still useful, and we can use it for whomever wants it or in certain circumstances," she replied. "So don't ever think that anything is a time waste here."

Sophia agreed, but she didn't even know what to say. It was just deflating. Here she was thinking she was doing something good and helpful, and instead she was developing software that the team would find intrusive and not nearly as useful as she thought.

Damon still stood behind them.

"I'm filing all the information from the dead guy they found," Sophia noted. "We've got the company name. We've got the financials. We've got all the email communications, texts, and phone records. I'm sending you a link, Damon, if you want access to any of it."

"Hell yeah. I want access to it all," he replied. "Good job."

Sophia was surprised at how much she needed to hear that. God, she was pathetic. This was not the time to be sitting here asking for kudos. Hell, she'd never asked for praise in her lifetime, so no way she would start now. She was good, and she knew it, so screw anybody who tried to make her feel anything less. Which really was nobody, just herself and her sudden lack of self-confidence.

Blowing the hair out of her face, she buckled back down again on the second Liverpool address of their possible hacker. She pulled all the property records, the city tax records, ownership records, and any financials related to it. "The current owner isn't a name that has popped up yet," she noted, "not so far anyway." And then she laughed. "And that's because the stated legal owner has been dead for years, his estate tied up in a lawsuit among family members, fighting over the will."

"Like we haven't seen that a time or two," Tasha replied. "You know that, if someone wanted to lay low, all they have to do is keep to properties caught up in court cases, like that one. A lot of the times they are sitting there empty because it'll eventually go to the heirs, and nobody even lives there, so people who don't want to be found could just move in."

"You think that's what was happening here?" Damon asked.

"Why not?" Sophia asked. "I'd certainly be checking out such properties, if I were looking to hide."

"Not only hide but assign everything to somebody else so it keeps you clean. It's not a bad thought process," Tasha admitted. She turned to look at Damon, who was buried in his laptop, reading through the info the women had gathered, absorbing everything. "Damon, did you hear her?"

He nodded. "I did, but how would somebody find that information?"

"Comparing obits to property records, court cases potentially," Sophia stated, frowning. "Other than that, I don't know. Maybe insight from an estate lawyer's perspective, who handles this kind of stuff, but then there's probably a lot of them out there. Tons of lawyers of all kinds." She shrugged. "I know that sounds thin, but it's worth a try."

"*Thin* doesn't matter," Damon replied. "What we need to know is how these guys are finding these places, who's involved, and why they are targeting us."

With the satellite feed up on Tasha's screen, Sophia looked over at her coworker. "I guess we're using a US government satellite for this one? Any chance they could track us?"

Tasha shook her head. "Nope, we aren't. We're using satellite access through Legendary Security." She looked at her and shrugged.

"Ah, I should have figured that. They've got great resources. Including Merk."

"Yep, it's nice to have connections to help get us emergency access to something like this," Tasha admitted. "We would have been up a creek without a paddle, starting from scratch with nothing."

Sophia shook her head. "There have been more than a few times I wished I'd had satellite access. Did you ever work with them on their satellite before this?"

"Never needed to. Stone was always there to help."

At that, Sophia laughed. "True enough, and he handles most of the security stuff. Anything needed is provided to you right off."

"I think more than a few people there are quite capable of helping him out now," Tasha noted, with a grin. "Anyway, at least we know that their satellite system is secure and solid."

"It is."

Right then a picture flashed up on the screen. "And we have one person approaching."

"Let's hope it's Merk," Sophia stated.

At that, Damon got up and stepped over to study the feed in front of them. Leaning forward, he asked, "It's really hard to tell, isn't it?"

"It is," Tasha confirmed, "and we can't get it any more accurate than that."

"It's already plenty accurate," he stated, "considering that we're so far away. It would just be nice if we could ID him for sure."

"Does he have our tracking on him?"

"No, Merk hadn't installed our tracker implant yet, and

Terk's been postponing it," Damon replied. "They've definitely talked about it, but Merk tends to stay closer to home these days."

"Right," Sophia agreed. "I guess that makes sense. He has got a family, doesn't he?"

"A wife … yes," he noted. "Levi has been bringing in new people and allowing some of the more senior ones to step back a bit."

"I don't think *senior* would be a word that either brother would like you to use in this case." Tasha smiled.

He grinned. "No, you're quite right there. That is likely to get me into big trouble."

"On the other hand, what we need is something completely different right now," Sophia noted. "We must track Merk, and I think we should use the resources we have." She quickly sent a text to Wade, asking how she was supposed to know if the man approaching the second Liverpool property was Merk. The response confused her. "He said he'd check." She turned and looked at the two of them and frowned. "What else am I missing? Can he actually do that from like thirty-five miles away?"

Damon looked at her, smiled. "This is where you just have to trust. Believe me. If anybody tells you more, it should be Wade himself."

Sophia opened her mouth and then slowly closed it. "More of that need-to-know stuff?"

"Not at all," he admitted. "It's just that the explanation would take a whole lot more time than we really can afford to spend right now," he murmured.

"Okay." She smiled. "As long as I'm not being shut out." Then she turned to watch the image on the screen. Her phone chimed with a simple text message from Wade.

Affirmative.

"Did he just call him? Is it that simple? Or am I being way too silly over all this spy stuff?"

"Nope," Damon replied.

"A phone call would be way too disruptive for these guys," Tasha noted. Sophia shot her friend a look, and Tasha added, "Later, Soph. Believe me, all of it will be explained later."

Sophia groaned. "Says you. It's all just frustrating as hell to be left in the dark."

"I know, and I'm sorry. But, as Wade shares more on this with you, you'll see for yourself."

"Yeah, I'll see, but I won't be able to help," she replied in frustration.

"No, you probably won't," Tasha stated, "and I'm sorry about that. We do what we can to support them. That is how we can help them for now, and there isn't time to go into the rest of it."

In her mind, Sophia had to wonder though. Could Wade really check out a location with his mind and somehow see somebody that far away? Was this the kind of extra skills the team worked with here? The possibility just amazed her. If it was even close to the truth, she really wanted to know more. She wanted to belong to something on the cutting edge, like this. And, with that thought, she had to laugh because, according to them, this wasn't cutting edge at all but old-school.

The problem was that people were coming after them, trying to take them out. Sophia was prepared to do her damnedest to make sure the bad guys didn't succeed. Just imagine if somebody could look through time or over great distances and see what *we* were doing? She shook her head.

"This shit is mind-boggling," she muttered.

But she kept her voice low and focused back on the work at hand. Because, of all the things that she needed to do, the most important was to make sure this man and this team stayed safe.

"HAS SHE FIGURED it out yet?" Terk asked Wade.

"Well, she knows a lot about it," Wade replied, as he and Terk finished the sweep of the Godwin family home in Liverpool. "I think she's confused but most likely not quite ready to accept the whole truth."

"She might surprise you," Terk replied. "Apparently some women don't have a problem with it."

"Yeah. Well, we already know that Tasha has come to terms with it. And, to a certain extent, Mera had accepted it too."

Terk asked him, "And you never really hit it off with her?"

"She was great to work with, but she wasn't anybody I saw myself spending time with," Wade noted. "She was a little nerdier than I can handle. When it's downtime, I want downtime. I don't want to be dealing with drama."

At that Terk nodded. "I'm 100 percent with you there," he agreed. "But you have to admit, we don't even know what downtime is." At the look on Wade's face, Terk swallowed a laugh.

They quickly exited Rodney's house and headed over to the other Liverpool location. "Do you want to contact your brother and see if he has found anything?"

Again a weird humming sounded in the vehicle. "He's

there, but I can't get any reading on his emotions," he replied, "so I rather imagine he's either still going through the place or doing reconnaissance."

"I'll drive, and you text him that we're on the way. Maybe give him a heads-up on any information we've grabbed so far. It's all interesting stuff, just not enough to really lock down anything yet."

"Nope, there'll be lots happening in that department yet. But the sooner we figure it out, the better."

"And I'm right there with you on that one," Wade agreed. "It's just frustrating." He drove carefully, completely ignoring everything Terk was doing because part of Wade's senses were off on a different corner. "Are you getting any kind of reading?" Wade asked after a few minutes. "Like from any of the other guys?"

"Not at the moment." Terk looked at him in surprise. "Why?"

"Because I'm getting a weird sense of somebody in the ethers."

"Love how you say that." Terk laughed. "As if it were a separate place."

"It feels like a separate place," he replied.

"To you … but it's also natural and integrated. For me, it feels like it's just one."

"Not me. It definitely feels like it's a separate place."

"Interesting," Terk stated.

"Feels like something's out there."

"Like a probe?"

"Like a probe … but not as efficient."

"Like somebody is hunting blindly?"

"Doesn't feel like a hunt though." He frowned, tilting his head. "It's hard to describe it."

"Do your best," he replied, "because we'll have to find it again later."

"Not that easy," he reminded Terk.

"Doesn't matter if it's easy or not. It's necessary," Terk stated. "You and I both know this is something we don't have an option on."

"I know. I know. But trying to track any of this stuff is almost impossible now." Wade didn't have the same control that Terk did, though Terk had often told Wade how he had a ton of unused power that he wasn't yet utilizing to the best of his ability. But that just made him frustrated because, if he could do more, why wasn't he?

"Still, you do have a ton more available. You just need to trust your instincts," Terk replied. "You still tend to reach out to people for the energy you need—which is very limiting because then you have to deal with all their issues while you siphon it off. Not to mention the guilt."

"And there you go, reading my mind again," Wade noted. "I thought we decided that wasn't cool."

"No, *you* decided it," Terk replied. "And, if you don't want me to read your mind, you should stop transmitting your every thought quite so strongly."

He groaned at that. "Only you would say something like that."

He burst out laughing. "Yep, and I could only really say it to you."

"Well, everybody else can do what I do, and that's why I've always wondered why I'm even on your team."

"Because you have the ability to do so much more. And believe me. I've never regretted having you on the team. A lot of people are good, but then some have the potential to be so much better."

"As long as I can get my shit together." Wade pulled the truck up to the proper address, and he looked around. "Doesn't look like anybody's around. I got a terrible feeling that we're up against another dead body."

"I wouldn't be surprised," Terk noted. "If they have something concrete … if they have a prototype … if they've actually activated this into human trials, they're probably taking out everybody who was involved in its development."

"Honestly I think our government probably would too," he offered.

"And I'm wondering if that isn't why we've been put down," Terk replied.

Wade turned and looked at him in horror. "Do you think our government developed this?"

"I don't know whether this was developed simply to get rid of us, or to see if these special skills exist in people, can we improve on it through technology and machines."

"I wouldn't be surprised if they have a sister program," Wade noted thoughtfully.

Terk frowned. "I mean, if they had any idea that this psychic software was doable, you know they'd be all over this. But I just don't think our government's doing this right now, no."

"Good," Wade snapped.

"Sometimes we just have to take some things on faith," Terk added. "And, although we know our government can act like a complete asshole, we're hoping it's not a 100 percent complete asshole." At that, he stepped out of the vehicle. "Now let's go find Merk."

CHAPTER 7

S OPHIA GOT THE text, confirming they were at the second Liverpool address, looking for Merk. She sent back a message, giving Merk's location according to the satellite. It's quite possible there was a lag on the satellite though, so she hoped they understood that. But, as she watched the dots on the screen match up and come together, she sat back with a sigh. "Looks like they found each other," Sophia muttered.

"Nothing less than what we'd expect," Tasha stated. "These guys are good."

She nodded. "And I know Merk. He's one of the best."

"How much have you actually worked with him?" Damon asked.

"Off and on for a while," she murmured. "Levi offered me a full-time job, but honestly I was still weighing my options, you know, with Wade."

"Even though he walked away from you?"

She nodded. "You don't find a connection that strong without being aware that the chances of ever finding it again are pretty slim," she noted. "So I know it makes me sound like I'm a complete stalker and an absolute loser, but I wanted to see him again to ensure that it really was a done deal and that he didn't need me."

"Well, I think he does, and I think you did the right

thing," Damon replied, with a smile.

"Maybe so, but we definitely need to take some time together to sort it all out."

"And yet how much sorting out to do is there?" Tasha asked, with raised eyebrows. "You moved into his room, and he didn't throw you out."

"Yeah, we just need that heart-to-heart conversation where we air it all out," she agreed. "He broke my heart, and I am aware that, at the moment, we're only here because I wanted that second chance. I don't think he would have sought me out, and that's something I have to live with. I've also got to wonder that, if things get tough again, will he walk?"

Damon and Tasha exchanged glances, and Sophia could tell they weren't exactly sure on the answer either. "It's not an easy thing to know that it's all good, but, if anything goes wrong, he may just decide to bail and not come home again."

"I don't think that's fair either," Tasha noted. "I know why he left, and I know why he didn't contact you. I get it, and I understand, and I wouldn't like it either. The thing about something like that is, once may be okay, then you clear the air, talk it out, and everybody understands. But once everybody is on the same page, doing that a second time would be completely unacceptable."

"Exactly." Sophia nodded. "So the trick is whether or not he gets that. Whether he's willing to stick around and to talk things out instead of doing another disappearing act," she noted.

With that, she pointed to the screen again. "So, now that these guys are actually together, who is this one?" As she spoke, she tapped on the screen a little bit farther up.

Immediately Damon swore. "Keep an eye on that one," he stated. "I'm warning them." In the background, she heard a message heading off to the guys, saying a bogey had just arrived.

Tensely, she watched as the men split up and headed off separately, as if to surround the new arrival. She wasn't sure she approved of the tactic, but that was the thing. She had enough field experience to know that sometimes there wasn't time to plan any more than that. With her heart in her throat, she watched as the men approached and then swiftly overtook the single man who'd arrived. "That was nice and clean," she noted in surprise.

"Why do you sound so surprised?" Damon asked.

"I figured they'd go down shooting."

"We don't know who the guy is," Damon reminded her. "It may just be some guy who owns the house and just came in after six months of traveling around the world."

She winced. "Oh God, could you imagine? You get home only to find out that your house was used in a multi-murder international incident."

"It has happened"—he nodded—"many times."

"Still, it just reminds me that people suck," Sophia replied, with a laugh.

"Absolutely, especially when it comes to this stuff."

As they watched, the four men now split up. Two went back to the vehicle and left the premises, and two stayed behind.

"Well, now what?" Sophia asked in astonishment. "I wasn't expecting this."

"And I don't particularly like it." Damon glared at the screen. He quickly picked up the phone and stepped off to the side. He returned moments later. "Good and bad news.

Merk found a dead body in the second Liverpool house, searched him, found no ID, no nothing. Merk's already left an anonymous tip with the local authorities. I've sent you the photo to ID."

Immediately Tasha and Sophia opened the attachment. Sophia gasped. "It's Randall Godwin."

"The guy from the conference?" Damon asked. She nodded. "The guy whose brother's been dead a few days in their family home?"

She nodded. "I suspect Randall was our initial hacker, trying twice to get into our system."

"Well, one less enemy hacker to worry about. Man, our bad guys continue to cleanup any witnesses." Damon shook his head. "Except for one. Wade is heading here with a prisoner, the guy wandering around outside the property where Randall Godwin was squatting."

"Okay, that could be our other hacker, the one trying to get into the team's trackers. But bringing a suspect here? That's not the smartest idea, is it?" Sophia asked. "He might have a tracker on him as well."

"Can you check?" Damon asked her.

"From here? It's like thirty-five miles between Manchester and Liverpool." She frowned, then thought about it. "Let's give it a good chance to find out." And she did a full-body scan, but the guys were so far away that it was hard to see the results. "I am having trouble, but maybe Terk or Wade can check."

"Maybe, but Wade has no energy, and he can't afford to use it for that right now," Damon noted. "And Terk isn't responding."

"He'll be using his energy to feed whatever safeguards he has put up around headquarters and the team," Tasha replied. "I really wish the guys hadn't split up."

Feeling a sense of urgency and unrest inside, Sophia grimaced. "I may use this stranger's tracker to send out a signal and see if it bounces."

"If that would do anything, go for it," Damon stated. "Because I'm not sure who this guy is."

"Did Wade say anything?" Tasha asked.

"Not much," he noted. "They didn't like bringing him here, but they couldn't keep him there, not without impacting their ability to search before the cops arrive." Damon paused. "Better if they could have just stayed there, but Merk already called in the dead body tip," he added, "and Wade is running low."

"Of course he is. He should be in his damn bed." Sophia's keys clicked furiously as she found the captive's tracker and set up a bouncing signal outward. "If somebody's transmitting on him," Sophia noted, "then there's a chance that I can find it and track it too."

"And if you're tracking it, I want you to backtrack it," Damon stated. "That's what it's all about, finding what the hell's going on here."

"Presumably this guy is secured in the vehicle," she added.

"Yes, but—"

Sophia knew exactly what the *but* meant. She worked furiously. "Bingo." And, with a ghost of a smile, she watched as a signal raced outward on her computer. "So he has got a tracker on him. He's being tracked and that means Wade can't bring his captive here."

"Got it." Damon sent the message to Wade. Then he stopped, looked at her. "Can you find out where the prisoner's signal is transmitted to, and then scramble it, so the bad guys can't find him?"

She looked up, smiled. "Way ahead of you," she replied. "I just don't know that I'll have time to get it done before they get here."

"I already warned Wade to take a detour." Damon's phone buzzed. "Terk, what's up?"

"Wade's energy signal is decreasing rapidly," he stated. "Can you help him?"

"Maybe," he replied. "Unfortunately I'm pretty low myself. Anybody else who we can use?"

"He needs somebody with a built-in pathway," Terk added, "which is why we're in trouble."

"Your energy too?" Damon asked, worried.

"It looks like Gage is waking up," Terk replied, "so that's taking my energy away from everybody right now. I'm trying though."

"Can you take from Merk?"

"I already have. But you know as well as I do that we can't take too much."

"We need more people on this team, damn it," Damon growled.

"Or …" Terk paused, "we need to find more traditional ways of working. And that would be rather stupid, considering the scale of work that we do."

"But only that kind of scale when things go right, and, at present, they aren't. Can you get Gage awake enough that he's not siphoning off you?"

"It'd be a mess if I tried. He keeps waking to the surface and then going back under again."

"Probably his subconscious telling him it's all FUBAR, and he should just stay under," Damon joked.

"The thing is, you know as well as I do that his instincts

are damn strong. So, if staying under will protect him, that's exactly where he'll be."

"Yeah, I know, but we also need him," he noted.

"He probably knows that subconsciously, but, to bring him in on something like this ... when he's already injured, it could kill him." And, with that, Terk disappeared.

"I have to try to send some energy to Wade," he told Tasha.

She looked at him in surprise. "Everything is energy," she stated. "Can't he just draw from anything?"

"If we were secured, yes, but, because we're trying to keep everything shielded, then not necessarily. It has to be those within the shield."

"Or *things* within the shield?" Tasha paused. "I know it sounds stupid, but can't he just draw energy, like, from a battery?"

Damon looked at her in surprise, and a smile peeked out. "Thank you. I needed that today." He looked back at Sophia, who was obviously listening. "So keep doing what you're doing. Try to lock on and track down who our prisoner is transmitting with. As soon as you get anything, you come and get me."

Sophia didn't even bother answering, but she knew that Tasha would. As soon as he was gone, she looked over at Tasha. "Okay, so I'll need a little more explanation than I've been given so far."

"Well, you know that they all use psychic abilities and that they all have something slightly different as far as skills. In this case, because they do missions as a group, Terk has shown them how to bolster each other's energy levels when they start to flag. And that can happen because they just burned it up, trying to get intel or on a mission themselves when they're starting to burn down," she stated. "Wade is not fully recovered and probably shouldn't even be out there." Tasha nodded at the look on Sophia's face.

Tasha continued. "He's struggling, plus he has been out there for a few hours and hasn't had a chance to recharge. Normally he would get some energy support from Terk, but one of our other team members is starting to wake up—Gage. He's fighting, and he's pulling a lot of energy because he's heavily injured and trying to heal. And that's making Terk's life a little bit harder because he has to keep track of his own energy flow too."

"Jesus, you make it sound like these guys have some sort of battery chargers."

"They are kind of like that for each other, but apparently they can take energy from various other things, if they're healthier and don't have all the security blocks on them that they have in place right now. And the blocks are there to stop people from tracking them, but we're not exactly sure how efficient that is."

"Well, we know that somebody found them," Sophia stated. "This guy from the conference—Randall Godwin, recently deceased. Last I traced him, he and his laptop were in Belgium. Obviously he's been on the move since then."

"Did you get his IP address?"

"Yes," she confirmed. "I'm checking back in and logging in to that computer. With any luck, I can stop the transmissions to our prisoner en route."

"Cut that connection fast," Damon snapped urgently, as he walked back in. "Wade is struggling, like I mean really struggling. If he goes down, his captive—depending on what abilities he might have or if he's not secured enough—could come after Wade."

Wide-eyed, Sophia reached the signal, and ended the connection to his captive with a final keystroke. "He's done," she noted.

"*Done*? Please tell me that we didn't just kill him outright?" Tasha blurted out.

"We shouldn't have, but I'm not exactly sure what else this tech is for," Sophia replied. "All I did was find a tracker connected to a receiver and cut the feed."

"And it's a good thing you did," Damon replied, "because keeping our team alive is paramount."

Sophia nodded. "I get that. I just wish I understood who this other team is."

"So do we," Damon agreed. "So do we." He gave her a sudden smile and added, "Find anything you can about that receiver's location."

"I'm on it." She was newly energized. If nothing else, it would keep her busy, so she would stop worrying about what was happening with Wade.

WADE FELT THE sweat beading on his forehead. He just had to make it back to base. He'd already put out a call to Damon and to Terk to see if anybody could help top off his energy but wasn't receiving a strong enough signal to know if anyone heard. Worst case scenario, Wade would have to pull over. That was the last thing he wanted to do when he was bringing back a prisoner. He wasn't even sure about the wisdom of taking him to their new base.

Surely they needed to have another place simply for questioning people, but right now another place was just more than they had access to or the ability to manage. He was grateful they were even secure at the current location. And that had only happened once Levi's group had gotten involved. It wasn't that the system Terk's team had always utilized was failing them; it just wasn't strong enough for the demands they were putting on it. Wade understood that; he really did, but right now it was just pure shit.

"What's the matter?" the kid beside him asked in alarm. "You really shouldn't be driving if you're not feeling good."

"Shut the fuck up," Wade snapped.

"Of course." The kid laughed. "You guys think you're something else, don't you?"

"Yeah, we do," he replied, hoping this kid would talk. "We can do all kinds of shit you can't do," Wade stated, pouring on a little bravado for good measure.

"No," the kid argued, "you're the dinosaurs. What you used to do and what you can do now, that's a very different story."

Wade stiffened at that. "So, I suppose you were behind all the attacks on my friends?" He glared at his prisoner.

The kid shrugged. "Old used-up guys like you, who needs them?" he asked. "Tech is the way to go these days."

"Maybe so," Wade admitted, "but tech still fails."

"Yeah, but not like you guys do though," he added, with a smirk. "Look at you. You can't even drive or get your head on straight," he noted. "I might be a prisoner for now, but will you keep up this charade?"

"Maybe not, but, if I die, don't worry. I'll take you with me."

"Like that's what I'm afraid of?" he asked in disgust. "Technology is always better."

"Nope, it sure hell isn't," he muttered. At the moment, Wade just needed to hold on, to keep going. Suddenly he felt an influx of energy coming his way, and he didn't even question where it came from or why. He immediately grabbed it and started filling his system. Sitting up straighter, he smiled. "I'm feeling better already."

"What the hell is *better*?" the kid asked, looking at him. "You still look like shit."

"Maybe so," he replied cheerfully. He should be worried about where that energy came from, since it wasn't normal for him to access energy just out of the blue like that. But somehow it came, and, for once, he hadn't argued. He would worry about it afterward, when all was safe and sound. He looked over to double-check that the prisoner was still secure. The thing was, this kid—hacker or not—couldn't have been a very big part of the whole outfit. Wade suspected that they had basically used this event as a chance to get rid of him. "You know they won't let you go back, right?"

"Shows what you know," he snapped. "I'm part of a team, and we leave no one behind."

Wade grinned at that. "If you say so. But, if you're on that team, trust me. You're expendable. Look at how easily we caught you, and no one is coming to save you."

"I've been hacking the best of the best for a very long time," the young man stated with arrogance. "You are the hack of a lifetime, and this will set me up for life."

"You can't walk away when you're done," Wade noted.

"If that's what you think, you're clearly not thinking straight," he argued. "They're on to you. You know that, right?"

"So you're one of the hackers who designed the system that tracked us? I presume Rodney was involved too."

"Rodney is our NSA asset," he stated. "I haven't spoken to him in a few days though. They had already sent somebody to check up on him." He shrugged.

This kid had no idea he was playing with fire. "Well, Rodney is dead," Wade stated bluntly. "Probably about three days ago."

The young man looked over at him in shock. "What do you mean Rodney is dead? Did you guys—"

"He's dead, like D-E-A-D, by a bullet straight through his forehead," he added. "Just found his brother Randall too, executed. What the hell did you expect?" Wade frowned at the kid, who looked worried now, as a sheen of sweat coated his forehead.

The kid shrugged, trying to hide his fear. "Not my deal. Rodney was fishing for more money all the time, and he didn't know how to keep his mouth shut."

"And of course you're much better than he was, right?"

"Damn straight. As long as they've got me, they don't even need him."

If Wade was getting to him, the kid didn't let on. "Are you really that stupid?" Wade asked in astonishment. "Don't you realize that you're next?"

"I'm not next," he argued. "I've got so much shit in progress with them. No way … You got it all wrong," he stated, "Rodney is the one who was the weak link. Of course he's dead. I told the asshole that he shouldn't be fooling around with upping the price and things like that, but he didn't want to listen. He was all about getting more money, and he said that we were being ripped off."

"But you didn't agree?"

"No, I sure didn't. I mean, it was a pretty sweet deal for us," he admitted. "Once you start thinking along those lines of greed, you know just no good comes of it."

"Well, you're right there," Wade agreed, with a headshake. They were almost back to base. "We're coming up to our location. I'll have to put a blindfold on you."

"Sure," he replied cheerfully. "It's not like the bosses don't already know where you guys are." That made Wade pause for a second, and the kid burst out laughing. "You should be worried," he noted. "Old techs like you, definitely disposable. New techs like me, definitely in high demand."

The trouble was, Wade also understood where this kid's bravado came from because, if you're a hacker in today's world, it did seem like the world was your oyster. It sucked, but Wade saw why, when these bloody kids were making millions doing nothing. Some of them were honest and upstanding citizens, but a lot of them were just pieces of shit.

But then Wade wasn't supposed to judge, at least according to what everybody kept telling him. He thought that was complete crap too. Just so much craziness was going on right now, and he wanted no part of it. At least he didn't want any part that would get him in trouble. That was the way of the world, and he thought it would always be this way. It was only with experience that these kids understood that nothing was forever.

Nobody cared or stayed long enough to make something sustainable. Already somebody was lining up behind you, pushing to get you out of the way. But Wade could tell this kid absolutely nothing—nothing that the kid would listen to. Wade just wanted to get him back alive, so they could ask him questions. The kid obviously had no problem talking, and that made him very valuable.

As they came up near the new headquarters location, Wade took a quick look around. "Doesn't look like we're being followed."

At that, the kid started to laugh. "Oh my God, you're

just so stupid."

Wade was having difficulty keeping his temper under control because he knew perfectly well that they hadn't been physically followed, but he was being digitally tracked, and most likely the kid was too. What Wade didn't know was if some failsafe would go off as soon as he got the kid inside. The last thing he wanted was to have this kid's head blow apart right in front of Sophia.

She still hadn't seen the uglier side of this work. Sure, she'd worked with Levi's group, but Wade had also checked in with Ice and had found out that, although Sophia was a hell of a field operative, she hadn't seen too much because she was working under contract, so she wasn't in on everything, which made a difference. She really didn't know what Terk did or what the rest of his team did. And Wade didn't want her to learn too much too soon to shock her. Truly he just didn't want to lose her.

How sad was it that he was even worried about something like that right now. So much shit was going on this very moment that he knew this wasn't the time or the place to start worrying about something like that, but, just like any other heartsick idiot in the world, her safety, mentally and physically, bothered him. It had been hard for him to walk away from her, and, by some miracle, she'd come back, so he didn't want to lose her now.

And he didn't want her to think that he was some bad guy, some terrible person. He *was* in a way, when his work required it at times, but really he wasn't. Confused and torn between raw emotions, he pulled into the car park several blocks away and yanked a blindfold from the glove box. He quickly secured it around the kid's head. "Now you might actually stay alive long enough to get inside."

"Of course I will," he stated fearlessly, "but you won't be alive much longer afterward."

Wade knew for sure, from all the bodies stacking up, that this kid really wouldn't live very long; Wade just wanted to get answers. Fast. They were on a clock, and he knew that. But the clock wasn't necessarily the one that this kid was thinking of. The kid thought that the bad guys would attack Wade's base because of the kid's own tracking information. The problem was that, although that might very well be possible, Wade also knew that the kid would get silenced first.

No way they wouldn't kill the kid. Part of their usual practice. Wade had seen this too many times and with too many cocky bastards like this. And the kid obviously didn't know jack shit about anything in terms of how the world really worked. For that, Wade was sorry because this kid was as good as dead. Wade turned, looked at him, and asked, "Have you made peace with your maker yet?"

"My maker is a piece of shit," he noted calmly. "I got a crappy deal right at the get-go. I made my life, so there is no point in giving credit to some asshole who put me on this planet, supposedly for my own good," he sneered.

At that, Wade nodded. "I get that," he noted. "But, when you go down, chances are you'll go way down. Just remember that."

The kid shrugged. "You live and you die. That's about the only thing I'm sure of in this world," he stated. "As long as you come to terms with the fact that you won't live past the next hour, it means nothing to me."

Wade nodded. "Good enough. Let's go meet the others."

"Can't wait." Wade pulled him from the vehicle. As

soon as they started walking, the kid asked, "Just tell me one thing. Did you really think that parking a few blocks away would stop anything?"

Wade really didn't, but, at the same time, it would slow somebody down. He couldn't feel anything out there, and that worried him too. As much as his energy was slowly recharging, he didn't have any way to know just how much additional energy was being filtered through—therefore, how much powered his senses, the original five and his extras. He sent a message to Terk. *Walking prisoner toward base. He's been making threats of an attack the whole way.*

He had a tracker, Terk responded. *Sophia and Tasha have dismantled that.*

But what if they didn't get it all or fast enough? Wade was extremely worried.

They're on alert, Terk replied, though he wasn't relaxed either. *Don't be surprised if your greeting when you arrive isn't exactly pleasant,* he joked, and Wade felt his boss's amused energy, though still thick with worry.

Hey, I am just glad to be home as always, Wade sent back, with a smile.

"You are awfully quiet," the cocky kid walking beside him stated. "I can imagine the empty, worried expression and that weird look in your eye. I mean, your silence is just such a dead giveaway."

"Yeah? Dead giveaway of what?" Wade asked, looking over at him.

"Brain fog. Do you even have enough strength to stop them?"

The energy comments were starting to piss off Wade, but, then again, that's probably what the kid wanted. "What are you?" Wade asked. "Eighteen?"

"Like hell," he snapped. "I'm definitely legal."

"Ah, I don't know about that," he replied. "I think you protest too much, are a bit on the immature side, I would say." Wade chewed his words and looked at the kid's lack of a beard. "You know what? I'll revise my original estimate. I don't even think you're eighteen yet. You're probably not a day older than seventeen, so maybe just on the brink of being legal."

"Oh, that would be so typical of you," he stated. "Judge a guy by his facial hair."

"Why not? You're judging by everything else."

"I judged by performance," the smart-aleck kid stated. "Nothing else in this world is worth judging a man by … You'll see … or maybe not," he quipped.

"Yeah, maybe or maybe not," Wade noted sadly. "What's your name, kid?" When he clammed up, Wade continued. "I'll just call you Ted. I'm sorry that you didn't rethink your options before it came to this." As they walked toward headquarters, Wade sensed a weird buzzing thickening the air. *Drone.* He looked over at the kid and frowned. "Are you okay?"

The kid shrugged. "Of course I'm okay," he stated, with a scoffing tone.

But Wade saw something going on. Something he didn't understand. He took a step off to the side and then another step. He pulled out his phone. "Just wait right there," he told the kid. "I need to make a call."

"Something bothering you? Oh sorry! Secrets and all that stuff."

He felt the kid's amusement, as Wade was rethinking this scene.

"What you guys don't know is that your bad guys are

already here."

Wade took two more steps away and then—seemingly out of nowhere—came a *ping*. As Wade watched, the kid's head flew back, and his body collapsed to the ground at an odd angle.

Followed a second later by a sharp pain in Wade's arm, even as he scrambled for cover.

CHAPTER 8

SOPHIA SCREAMED AND bolted to her feet, grabbing her arm, feeling a weird pain radiating down it. She looked around frantically.

Tasha immediately hopped up, grabbed Sophia by her shoulders, and softly shook her. "What's the matter?"

Sophia stared at her in shock. "Didn't you hear that?"

"Hear what?" she asked, giving her friend a headshake.

Sophia took a slow deep breath, as Damon came toward her, his gaze intense.

"Didn't you feel any pain?" Sophia frantically asked him.

He nodded slowly. "I did. What did you hear?"

"I don't know. A muffled sound and a pain in my arm," she stated. "It's hard to describe."

"Yeah, that describes it pretty decently."

Tasha looked at Damon in surprise, and he just gave a tiny shake of his head. Tasha shrugged. "I didn't hear it, sure didn't feel it, and I don't know what you're talking about, but, whatever it is, let's hope it's not our guys in trouble."

"It is." Sophia raced to the rear door. "It's Wade."

"Hold on, hold on." Damon grabbed her good arm. "We don't just go bolting out there like that."

She stared at him but felt the panic rising in her throat.

"I know," he agreed. "I feel it too. Let's just calm down. We'll find him." Just then his phone vibrated; he checked the screen. "That's him now." Damon answered the call. "Wade, what happened?"

Damon listened, his gaze going to Sophia. "Yes, I know. I heard it too, a weird *ping*." He nodded. "Yeah, okay, fine. Can you get back in here without being seen? I know ... I know. We'll get the cops looped in," he replied. "I don't know what else we're supposed to do. Without having the US government to back us on this, I'm afraid MI6 will start thinking we're responsible for all these bodies."

He listened again, while the two women stared.

"Well, they'll twist it that way, if they don't know the truth," he added. "Come on in. We're ready and waiting for you." He immediately disconnected the call. "The kid Wade was bringing back had his head blown off just outside ... Wade thinks it was a drone, probably tracking him."

"That's impossible. I shut down the kid's tracker," Sophia argued. "They must have had a visual already because I'm certain that tracker was out of the equation."

"Unfortunately that's quite possible," Damon replied. "Wade seems pretty upset about the deal, as I guess the kid was only about seventeen."

Both women gasped. Sophia was horrified and bewildered. "That's just pathetic," she cried out. "Why would they be using someone so young?" Then she stopped, winced. "Oh God, he's got to be a hacker ... The one trying to get into our trackers."

"And likely completely so full of himself that he didn't realize he was disposable," Damon noted.

Just then came a series of alarms.

Sophia raced over to her console and muted the blaring sound. She looked at Damon and shrugged. "I just shut it down, to allow Wade entry, but surely you have a better protocol than that."

"We have lots of protocols in place," he replied. "It's not an issue this time."

As she watched the rear door finally opened, Wade stepped inside. Sophia saw the fatigue and the anger on his face. She raced over and threw herself in his arms. Nobody was happier than she was when his arms wrapped securely around her and held her close. "I'm so sorry," she whispered. "So damn sorry."

He nodded and just kept holding her. Finally he stepped back ever-so-slightly. "They just shot him, Damon. They just opened fire on him. Assholes. The kid—I mean, he couldn't even have been seventeen," Wade stated. "He couldn't even grow a beard yet because he was too young." He sat down on the closest chair. "His body is just out there. I left it. I did take off the bandanna, but anybody who is tracking would have seen it."

Sophia was upset at the blood on his arm. She quickly checked it out, cleaned it up, relieved when she saw it was just a burn. "They were tracking him, but I shut down his tracker. But they probably had enough of a visual already."

"A drone." Wade nodded. "Run by somebody with a decent aim and some drone operation experience, who knew what they were doing. The kid was targeted, and they took him out." Wade shook his head. "Instead of getting better"—he turned to face Damon—"things are going to shit."

"Not completely," Damon replied. "The good news is that Gage is starting to wake up."

At that, Wade bolted to his feet, joy on his face. "Seriously?" he asked. "I've avoided trying to look in that direction just because of the drain on my own energy. Speaking of which, I need food, and then I have to collapse."

He looked over at the food table and took a few unsteady steps forward. "Shit, looks like that unexpected energy surge is gone." And, just like that, he collapsed.

CHAPTER 9

DAMON SWEPT THE exhausted Wade off the floor and carried him to his room. He lay Wade down on his bed.

Sophia followed along behind. "Is this really just exhaustion?" she asked Damon in a low voice.

He nodded. "Yes, that's exactly what it is. He shouldn't have been out as it was. And definitely for not that long."

"But we won't tell him that, will we?" she asked, with a knowing look.

"Nope, absolutely not," Damon agreed. "We're all doing the best we can. Unfortunately the enemy has got us on the run, and all we can do right now is try to keep ahead of them."

"We're getting there," Sophia stated. "I know it doesn't always seem that way, but we really are."

"We just need to get ahead of them a little more," he added. "So we're not pushing ourselves to the very limits and then collapsing like this." Damon stared at Wade, still out. "Are you staying in here?"

She was torn.

"He'll be out for at least an hour," Damon replied, "and he'll need food as soon as he wakes up."

"And I'm not even sure we have enough," she muttered. "It's not like we're ordering in deliveries, are we?"

"We'll have to make a run."

"That doesn't sound good either," she noted, frowning. "It seems like we're being watched one way or another. Now that they took out their tracker-hacker guy with a drone right in front of our place, that makes us sitting ducks."

Damon nodded. "I can run a certain amount of shielding," he stated, "but I can't do it for long."

"But we also can't survive without sustenance. And he's a proof of that." Sophia nodded toward the collapsed Wade.

"No, I agree." Damon nodded. "Somebody like you may have to go because they don't know you."

"I'm not sure that they *don't* know me," she replied cautiously. "I just came on board, and there is good chance they may not know I'm working for you. But, if anybody knows that I was part of Merk's team at Ice and Levi's compound, that's a different story."

Damon frowned. "It might be a chance we have to take," he noted reluctantly.

"I get it … It's not like a shopping cart can hit me back, right?" she asked jokingly. "I probably look a little homeless just now anyway."

"Not necessarily a bad disguise at that," he admitted.

"Except the homeless aren't usually spending hundreds on groceries," she stated. "No arguing with that." No way to ignore the fact that these men had to be fed. Maybe more so if they were unraveling, as far as their abilities went, but they were definitely in need regardless. "Although we might minimize the risk. Can we have Merk pick up everything we need and do a handoff or something?"

Damon was reluctant to share the idea, but he relayed it to Terk. "That will really bring his brother into the picture, And we're trying to keep him more as a hidden weapon."

"Got it," she agreed, "so it falls to me. Do we have wheels?"

He nodded. "But they're several blocks away."

"Good, so I don't come out of hiding and immediately walk to a truck parked in front of our new headquarters. That would give me away for sure. However, it'll take quite a while to unload a huge stash of groceries back and forth, if I need to park blocks away at another location. But we can do this," she agreed. "And, if we get enough food today, we won't have to shop again for another few days or so."

"Feeding five of us or possibly even six soon," Damon noted reluctantly, "will be a bigger challenge."

"Well, if we're bringing in more people"—she frowned at him—"I presume you mean another team member or two. If so, they better bring food with them." Sophia chuckled at her own joke. "I'll go get what we need for now, and we need to plan another forty-eight hours ahead to do a repeat. You and I both know that it takes good food—of the perishable type—in order to get through something like this."

"It does," Damon agreed. "Most people really don't think along those lines."

She shrugged. "We have things that must be done, and they need to be done now, so it's all good as far as I'm concerned."

He smiled and nodded. "Let's figure out where the closest high-end store is, get a meal plan made up, and get some groceries brought in."

"On it." She walked back to her station to find Tasha still working away like crazy. "Tasha, what do these guys like to eat?" she asked. "I need to do a grocery run."

Tasha looked at her and frowned. "Are you sure that's

wise?"

"Wade alone will need more food than we've got," Sophia noted, "and, when he wakes up, he'll be hungry."

Tasha made a funny face. "You haven't seen anything like what these guys can put away when they need energy," she replied. "They make me look like a lightweight, and I'm no slouch when it comes to eating."

"So, I'm not wrong. We will need food and a lot of it."

"Yep, sure," she agreed. "Get proteins bars, whey, eggs, lots of sliced meats, bread …" And, with that, they set up a grocery list and a meal plan. When she looked at it, Tasha winced. "It'll definitely take a few trips."

"And that's not a problem. Well it is, and it isn't because we don't have wheels that can come up to headquarters."

"Right," Tasha murmured. "Well … let me know when you're close, and I'll do what I can. Maybe I can come out and give you a hand."

"I don't think the powers that be would agree with that." Sophia chuckled. "But it's all right. We'll figure this out. First, I need to go get the groceries." And, with that, she shot a look at Damon. "I hate to be so basic here, but what am I supposed to pay for the groceries with?" He opened his wallet and pulled out a bigger stack of cash than she'd ever taken grocery shopping before. "Wow. Okay, this is obviously good news," she replied. "I was afraid I would have to rob the store in order to get what we need."

"Would you have?" he asked curiously.

She shrugged. "If I had to? Absolutely. Would I want to? No, but, when the chips are down, absolutely no place to go but up. Unfortunately that's just the cost of doing business when you're under attack. Of course I would go back afterward and pay them"—she shrugged—"but that's just me. I doubt everybody would."

He laughed. "Well, rest assured that we absolutely would," he noted, "but, so far, that's not an issue. I'll have to get more cash for if and when Gage arrives."

"If Gage will be in the same shape as Wade here, he might be better off staying where he is."

"Oh, no doubt about it," Damon agreed, with a smile. "You just don't understand that these guys don't like to stay put."

"No, but I'm beginning to realize that." Sophia sighed. "Okay, I'm heading off." So, with that, and directions on how to get to the vehicle, she grabbed keys, a hoodie, a scarf, and a collapsible pushcart that she'd found at the back of the warehouse in which she put several reusable carry bags.

He looked at her and asked, "Are you okay with that?"

"Well, I'll be okay until I'm not," she stated. "I wasn't kidding when I said that, if we're bringing in this amount of food, I'll need to do a few trips." He frowned, as she shook her head. "Don't worry about it," she added. "It's not a big deal. It's just something that exposes us and that we must be aware of."

He nodded at that. "I get that. Stay safe."

She smiled. "Always." With that, she slipped out. She made her way to the vehicle, got it started right away, and then, following the GPS instructions, she headed to the grocery store. If anybody found the vehicle and took it from her, that would be a problem because they would have a good idea where she'd come from. She was tempted to wipe it and then realized that, for the moment, she would need it—plus, she didn't want to wipe it without permission. But still, she was part of this operation too now, and this lack of shared info was really bugging her.

When she got to the storefront, she sent a text message. **I'll wipe the GPS, should the truck be gone when I come back out.** She got a thumbs-up, so that's what she did, completely clearing its history. Next she headed inside the grocery store, grabbed a big shopping cart and started through her list. It would take a bit of time, which she knew, but that was part of being human these days. You had to eat.

It also made for a visible weakness because anybody could follow her and could figure out where she was coming from and how many people she was feeding with all this food. Short of her setting up for a long siege, clearly she was buying for well more than just her. Buying food for more than one wasn't the issue. Buying food for more than four or five would have curious eyes on them.

By the time she was finished, she knew she would make more than two trips to unload all this. If she packed this up and carried the excessive weight in one trip, it would put Sophia in more danger of attack than by being out for a second trip. Frowning, she went through the checkout lane and headed back to the vehicle, happy to see it was still where she had parked it. As she hopped in, she quickly sent a text, letting Damon know that step one was complete.

As she headed out of the parking lot, she watched, seeing another vehicle pulling out behind her. She studied the license plate, memorizing it, and, at a stop sign, quickly texted the license plate number to Tasha.

Almost immediately Tasha replied. "It's a tail. You'll have to lose it."

"Yeah, I got that," And Sophia did. She hadn't been working in this industry for such a short time that she didn't know what kind of trouble they were heading into. At the same time, she didn't want to be the one who brought anybody back to their base.

Heading toward a parking mall and moving around through to the loading zones in the back, she passed by several semitrucks, unloading and loading, before heading back around on the opposite side. But, of course, having completely ditched the GPS data, she had to punch in new coordinates.

At the same time, Tasha texted her and gave her directions.

And, with that, Sophia returned to where she'd first located the truck, near their base. She called Tasha. "Your directions worked. I'm here. I'll be inside in a little bit."

"Take your time, and make sure you're not being followed."

"I got that," she replied. "It's not so much about being followed at this point, as these multiple trips will make it a little more suspicious."

"I know," Tasha noted. "We're working on a solution at our end."

"Not too much of a solution to be had for now, since we've got one down and the other isn't nearly strong enough yet."

"I hear you," Tasha stated. "I could come out and help though."

"Nope, I can do it myself. I just don't want to overload it too much each time," she noted. "Plus, I did grab a little pushcart, so I'll disguise myself as homeless, and we'll see how I do—keeping all senses open, looking for issues." By the time she made it to the door with the first load, it opened before she could knock. She immediately passed over this load and then turned and walked back, not wasting any time. Keeping an eye out around her was also paramount.

As soon as she was out in the open air, she immediately adopted the persona of a bent-over slightly older woman, plodding slowly but carefully along, as if afraid of falling. By the time she returned to the vehicle, she felt a vibration of a text that she looked at surreptitiously.

Looks like you're in the clear.

She didn't really trust it, and her instincts said it wasn't trustworthy either, but she also knew that she had to keep moving forward, hoping all was good. By the time she had the remainder of the groceries all packed in her pushcart, she turned and started to walk again.

Halfway to headquarters, a truck pulled up, and two men stepped out in front of her.

She looked at them. "May I help you?" she asked in a polite tone of voice.

"Absolutely," one of the young men replied. "Where are you going with those groceries, Grandma?"

She didn't flinch. "Well, my thought was to take them home, where they belong," she stated, with a note of humor. "Isn't that what most people do with groceries?"

"Aren't you too old to be lugging so much?"

"What are you doing, rationing me?" she asked, looking around. "Not all of us can afford two, three trips to the market at this age."

He hesitated. "You don't look that old."

"You're the one calling me *grandma*," she replied. "What would you like me to respond with?" She kept pushing forward, and the two men fell into step beside her. "What's your problem that you're hanging around with me?" she asked, trying to make her voice quiver slightly. Which wasn't hard, given the circumstances. "Surely some pretty young ladies are out there who you'd rather spend time with."

"Absolutely there is," the more belligerent one stated in a derogatory tone. "Too bad I don't get that opportunity right now."

She shrugged. "So you're just here, hassling a helpless old lady. Interesting life choice."

"We're not hassling," the other guy replied, his tone a little affronted at her accusation.

"Well, it's not like you're here because you want to be here," she replied. "You're here because you're up to no good." She probably shouldn't egg them on, but waiting for them to do something was nerve-racking.

She knew perfectly well that she was being watched on satellite back at headquarters; she just didn't know how real-time it was. She could hope it was within seconds, based on what she'd seen so far, but there was always the chance that maybe it wasn't quite that current. Or that the team wasn't exactly seeing what she was experiencing. She proceeded at an even slower pace, until the men got impatient.

"I just want to know where you're taking all those groceries," the guy repeated, laughing at her.

She stopped and glared at him. "Why?" she asked. "I don't like seeing thugs finding out where I live."

At that, he burst out laughing. "It's really not a problem, Grandma … You're hardly anything anybody wants."

"But apparently I'm somebody you guys just want to hassle."

He shrugged. "Why not? I didn't have anything better to do today."

"That's all there is in your life?" she asked. "Nothing better to do in your day, so let's go give this old lady a hard time?" She looked over at other one. "Is that who you guys are? How very sad."

He glared at her. "You're hiding something. There's way too much food here for you."

"It's exactly because of guys like you that I don't shop very often."

"Have other people hassled you?" he asked in surprise.

"What? You think you're special now?" she asked, with a shake of her head. "Somebody's always out there trying to take from others," she stated. "That doesn't make you special at all."

"We aren't trying to take your food," one of them replied, affronted at the accusation. "I want to know who you're feeding. We're looking for some guys."

"Looking for some guys?" she asked and then gave a hard shake of her head. "I don't even know what that means."

"Doesn't matter," he replied. "We'll just follow along and see where you go."

"*Great*," she muttered under her breath, but, sure enough, they fell behind ever-so-slightly. It was one thing for her to disappear quickly; it was another thing for her to disappear with the load of groceries. Just then a vehicle came slowly driving up. The driver looked at the two guys near her, a hard look on his face, as she looked over at them.

"Friend of yours?" she asked, as she tried to deflect. "He took pictures of you." The thugs looked at her in surprise, then turned to look back at the vehicle. "The driver took photos of your faces." She laughed. "Sounds like you're not the only one out hunting."

They both looked at her for a long moment and then fell back. When she turned around again, they were gone. She sped up and headed into a completely different area of the block and waited. When she got an **All clear** text from Tasha, Sophia proceeded around to the rear door. "Wow," she replied, "those guys followed every step I took."

"Which is why Damon went out in that truck," Tasha noted.

"I didn't even know we had a truck like that."

"We don't," she admitted cheerfully. "He lifted it."

"Good enough," Sophia replied. "That was enough to send them off. Did you guys get photos?"

"Yep, we were taking photos of them, not that we necessarily wanted them to know about it."

"Oh, I think it was a good thing that they were notified," she agreed. "They were up to no good."

Tasha nodded. "But they were just punks, weren't they?"

"Yeah, punks wanting to be tough punks. I think they were hired to find out who I was and what I was doing."

"Which is also concerning."

"But we should have expected it anyway," Sophia noted. "The drone was in this area, and we have to expect that it'll keep up surveillance around here, even after they shot the hacker kid."

"Or, instead of street bullies, they could have sent another drone back," Tasha stated. "It's probably a given at this point."

"And you can't blame them for trying, I guess."

WHEN WADE WOKE up, his body was soaked in perspiration. That was a new symptom, and he wasn't sure he liked it much, but, given what he'd been through, it wasn't shocking. Still, it was concerning since it was different. He sat up, pushed back the bedcovers, and headed toward the shower. Almost immediately the bedroom door opened, and

Sophia stepped in. "You okay?" she asked abruptly, as she moved toward him.

He shrugged and nodded. "I've been better. I was just going to take a shower." He motioned at his skin. "I'm soaked at the moment."

She nodded. "Okay, food'll be ready when you come out."

"Oh, good … Did somebody go get some?"

She smiled and nodded. "Yeah, I did." He froze, then a moment later, he spun around to look at her, and she shrugged. "Hey, somebody had to."

Nodding, obviously not liking that she took that risk, he closed the bathroom door and stepped under the hot water. Not a whole lot to like about any of this, and, if everybody had to step up and contribute, he was glad that she offered. The fact that she was already back meant that there hadn't been any trouble, and, for that, he was damn grateful. By the time he was washed, showered, scrubbed clean, and had the bedding changed, something that he managed to do himself, he stepped out of his room, feeling better.

"I don't know how long the energy will last," he admitted lightly, as he felt Damon's watchful gaze, "but I'm doing okay."

"Good." Damon nodded.

"What about Terk? Where's he at?"

"He's on the way back now. He met up with Merk, and they've done some extra planning—but I don't really know anything about it yet."

"Well, you will now," Terk replied, as the door opened. They all looked at him in surprise.

"What the hell?" Sophia asked, as she bolted to her feet. "I had safeguards in place."

He gave her a gentle look. "That's good. Keep them there." Then he walked over to the table and set down the box he had in his arms. "Damon, you want to come give me a hand? I've got a little bit more to unload." With that, the two men disappeared.

"Where is he parked?" Sophia asked.

"I don't know." Tasha jumped up and strode over to the table, looking at the boxes. "Electronic equipment," she noted, with a nod. "That makes sense."

"What doesn't make sense though is how he got in. Did somebody crack through my system?" Sophia asked in a panic.

At that, Tasha placed a gentle hand on her shoulder. "Calm down."

She looked at her, frowned, and asked, "Why would I? Why are you guys not panicking too?"

"Because it's Terk. And, if you realize one thing here, it is that his abilities go way beyond what anybody would expect."

"So you're telling me that he used some sort of woo-woo powers to do this?" she asked, with a wave of her hand.

At that, Damon laughed, as he came in, packing a box. "That's a good way to look at it … Yes, that's exactly what he did. And he's damn good at it."

"So he can get in and out without triggering an alarm?" Sophia asked in shock.

"That and so much more," he admitted, nodding.

"Okay." Sophia frowned. "I can't say I feel terribly secure with that fact. I mean, if he can do it, how many others can?"

"Well, hopefully … none. But that's what we need to figure out," Damon noted. "It's one thing to have a comput-

DALE MAYER

erized tracking system … It's another thing entirely to have somebody who can walk through alarms."

"Please don't tell me that he can walk through walls too," Sophia scoffed, only half-joking, but she searched both their faces intently.

Wade just smiled and shook his head. "Not that I know of."

"That's not exactly a *no* though, is it?" Sophia muttered.

Damon grinned. "No, it sure isn't. You are new, but, in this industry, you've got to understand that nothing is ever for sure. Nothing is ever stagnant. It's constantly changing and evolving, just as our abilities are."

And, of course, she really wanted to bite the bullet and to ask him more about his abilities, but, just then, Terk returned again. "Did you park close by?"

He nodded. "I had too much to bring."

She rolled her eyes. "Yeah, I did too. So I made several trips."

He nodded casually. "We all do what we can do."

She wasn't sure if he meant that, since she didn't have any exceptional abilities, this is what she could do, or because he did, he had other options. Either way, she figured it was better off not to ask again. She sighed and sat down at the computer to make sure that everything was otherwise running properly. She was really bummed that he hadn't set off any alarms, and that was just damn freaky.

She would have a talk with Merk one of these days, when *whatever the hell this was* got over and done with and when they had a moment. Although, as she thought about it, Merk probably wouldn't tell her jack shit anyway; it was his brother, Terk, after all. And his twin at that. If Merk had to do something to keep his brother safe, it was a given that he would.

It wouldn't matter what she wanted to know or what anybody else had to say, and she'd agree with that. She didn't have any siblings and was raised by her grandparents, and their bond was something special. Merk wouldn't betray his twin brother or share information that would put Terk at risk for anything.

Wade sat down at the table, assessed the food selection, and made himself a big sandwich. He cut into the French bread, taking half of it as part of his sandwich. By the time he had his sandwich made, he felt his strength waning again. Deciding he had had enough of this BS, he started to eat and worked his way through the entire thing pretty damn fast. When he looked up, Sophia stared at him in astonishment. He shrugged. "Hey, I was hungry."

"Well, now I can see why we'll have to get groceries again so soon. At this rate, we'll need them fast," she joked.

He nodded, with a smile. "Particularly for people like us. When we're burning through a lot of calories," he noted, "it's always a challenge to keep the supplies stocked."

"It wasn't such a challenge," Tasha remarked from behind them, "when we actually had a full support. Now it's a different story entirely."

"Did you have any problems when you were out?" he asked Sophia. When an odd silence came, he looked up and felt something in his heart congealing. "You did ... What happened?" he asked immediately.

Sophia shrugged. "I'm sure you could see a copy of the satellite feed, if you want to take a closer look at it," she suggested. "Basically two guys hassled me, and then, when it looked like I was having a hard time ditching them"—she pointed at Damon—"he came driving by, very obviously taking photos of them."

Wade's eyebrows furrowed. "*Huh.*"

"As soon as they thought they were being photographed," Damon added, "they immediately faded away."

"We figured that the drone gave them a general location for us, and, since I had such a big load of groceries," she noted, in a dry tone, looking over at Terk, "I think they may have thought I had too many groceries for a single person."

He nodded slowly. "I'm sorry."

She shrugged. "Remember. I worked for Levi's team on several ops," she noted, "although not in a full-time capacity."

"I know, and I'm not suggesting you aren't capable. I'm just not happy that you were put in that position," Terk clarified.

"Well, you can't always protect me, just as I can't always protect you," she stated, with a flat glance Wade's way.

Wade frowned as he thought about that and agreed. "That's just the way of life, isn't it?" he muttered. "Wouldn't it be nice if we could do something more about it?"

"Wouldn't it," she agreed, "but the chances of that happening anytime soon aren't that great."

There wasn't a whole lot Wade could say to that, so he just nodded and kept on eating. He was on his second sandwich and hungrily eyeing the rest of the French bread.

"Seriously?" she asked.

"Did you happen to pick up any peanut butter?"

She got up and walked over to the bags on the counter and pulled out two jars.

"Perfect," he stated. "I gather Tasha told you about that."

"Yeah, you seem to have this thing about peanut butter."

"It helps me regenerate quickly." Wade laughed.

She watched as he took two big slabs off the French bread and quickly smothered them in butter and peanut butter. When he started eating them, almost as rapidly as he had the sandwiches before, she stared. "Do you need more food?" she asked. "Because, if that's the case, I can cook something." But then she stopped, looked around. "Or not? We don't really have much in the way of facilities to do any real cooking here, do we?"

"No need to cook on my account," Wade replied. "We'll be fine. I just need to tank up again."

Sophia nodded, not entirely convinced that she was getting the whole story from him. But, when she looked over at the others, they were already deep in thought, and she figured nobody would explain things. At least not yet. She looked over at Tasha, who was busy on the computer again, so Sophia joined her there. "And he always eats like this, right?" she asked Tasha. "So there's no reason to worry?"

Tasha immediately nodded. "No need to worry. Peanut butter is always his go-to food, especially when we're short on options."

"Right, so no steak barbecues anytime soon."

"Nope, none, nada." Tasha laughed. "Let go of your dreams of having anything fancy for a while."

"It doesn't really matter." Sophia shrugged. "As long as there's enough food that we're not starving and that we can keep their energy up."

"Exactly."

And, with that, Wade, who'd been listening in, reached for an apple and said to Tasha, "Send me the satellite feed of when Sophia went for the groceries, please." Tasha did so without question, but Sophia looked at him and frowned. "I might recognize them," he explained easily.

Sophia wasn't sure that she believed him, but then, as she thought about it, it was exactly what she would be doing if their roles were reversed. When he put down the peanut butter jar the next time, she asked, "Are you good with that video now?"

"Looks like they were just a couple punk kids."

"Well, older than that by a few years and ones with an agenda, but they weren't pros."

"Next time they're likely to be that much more aggressive," he noted.

"Agreed, but hopefully by then, we'll be dealing with a completely different scenario. And, with any luck, I won't be alone."

He frowned, then nodded. "Let's hope so."

"And remember. This is the job I'm doing too. You can't just protect me because you want to."

"Of course I can. But you won't really allow me to." And, with that, he got up and walked over to join the men. Really no point in arguing about it. He was still confused and tired, but they needed a plan. Wade looked at Damon. "Did you track down those two punks?"

"Yeah, I did," Damon stated. "They both live in a halfway house on Kirkland Avenue."

"Let's go have a talk with them," Wade suggested.

Damon agreed, then looked over at Terk. "You need to stay and recharge."

"Absolutely I do," Terk agreed, without argument. "And you guys need to not do anything stupid."

"Well, they're the ones who started it." Wade's temper rose at the reminder.

But both men looked at him and shook their heads.

"Absolutely no way will this come to blows," Terk ordered. "You need to keep your emotions out of it. We need intel, not trouble."

"I'll get it out of my head," Wade replied, "when some semblance of normalcy returns. In the meantime, they're on my shit list." And, with that, he turned and walked out, not waiting for Damon.

CHAPTER 10

"**H**EADS-UP," TASHA SAID to Sophia, as the men disappeared.

"What's up?"

"They're going out to talk to those young guys who hassled you on your way home with the food," she explained. "Terk will go on his Energizer Bunny shift, and we're to track the men on satellite." Tasha immediately opened up the satellite feed and watched as the two men headed out.

"So it's just me who had to keep hiding and parking a long way away?" Sophia asked in disbelief.

"Not necessarily," Tasha stated. "What you don't realize is that these guys also have the ability to shield themselves to a certain extent."

"Yeah, I don't know any of this stuff." Sophia reached up a hand to rub at her temple. "But, as long as you guys think you've got it covered, then fine."

"We haven't got anything covered," Tasha admitted. "Otherwise we wouldn't have been taken down like we were. But we're getting to the bottom of it."

"Says you," Sophia huffed. "I think we've just landed in chaos and a whole lot more confusion instead of answers."

"Well, I really hope you're wrong," Tasha admitted, "but you know what? We've all been stuck on this one, and none of us is really sure what's happening, so we'll figure it out. That's the bottom line. We don't know now, but we will find out."

"Good enough," Sophia replied and watched her screen, as the men headed down the road. "And they'll go find these two guys?" she asked.

"Yep, they were paid by somebody."

"If I'd have really thought about it, I could have taken them down myself and maybe brought them back in." She looked around the room. "I just didn't think that's what I was supposed to be doing."

"It wasn't," Tasha agreed. "And you probably could have, but it was more important that we follow protocol."

"Yeah." Sophia still felt like she had missed out on an opportunity though. And she felt disappointed in herself that she didn't take any proactive measures. Why the hell hadn't she thought of that? That was just BS that she'd missed that chance. She felt herself getting angrier by the second.

Finally she got up and walked over to make herself a sandwich, and when she came back, Tasha was staring at her.

"Feeling better?"

She groaned. "I guess you guys are all supersensitive to how people are feeling, huh? I suppose you have to be, living in close quarters like this." She shrugged. "I'm mostly just angry at myself."

"It's normal to react that way, especially after the fact, but it really wasn't the thing to do at the time, so it's good that you didn't."

"Says you," she muttered. "I feel like it's something they might have expected me to do."

"Nope, not at all." Tasha really wanted Sophia to understand that it was not only *not* expected but it wouldn't have been desired, if she'd pulled it off. "Listen. Right now these guys aren't used to having any help at all," she explained, as Sophia looked at her sharply. "It's not that they don't want our help." She shrugged. "They have their team, and that's all they've been used to having for a very long time," she stated. "Anything other than that is just gravy."

"Yeah, well, I don't want to be thought of as *gravy*," Sophia stated. "I've done a lot of missions. Not full-on heavy action, like maybe they would expect if I were to say that, but, at the same time, I wasn't sitting there twiddling my thumbs either."

"Good," Tasha replied, "because right now we'll need all hands on deck."

"You think those kids were bad news?"

"What do you think?" Tasha asked. "You met them."

"I think they were punks, who could be pushed to do a whole lot more, but they were uncertain. As they gain confidence, they will become a pain in the ass to whatever law enforcement is around here."

"Right," Tasha agreed. "Well, let's see how the guys do with them."

"And what about Terk?" she asked, as she looked around.

"He's gone to lie down."

"Can he really just recharge like that?"

"Nope, not necessarily. He's burning through an awful lot of energy right now."

"Yeah, Wade was evasive about it, something about the other guys," Sophia stated.

"So the answer to that question is *maybe*, but it would potentially be much more difficult right now."

"Which really means, you have no idea."

Tasha laughed. "You know what? That's not a bad assessment," she agreed. "I can speculate, since I've worked close to Terk for a long time, but I really don't know. This situation is completely unprecedented."

"Yep."

Together, they watched the satellite feed as Damon and Wade drove, but they didn't go very far. When they did pull off into a side area, Sophia immediately marked it and started assessing ownership of the properties in the area and who was registered at the halfway house. "We have two guys," Sophia noted, "who checked in just two days ago."

"That'll be them," Tasha stated cheerfully. "If you've got names, send it in a text to the guys."

Sophia did that immediately. When she got a response back from Wade, asking if anybody else had been there long-term, she immediately assessed the rest of the residents. She sent him the information that she had and waited to hear a reply. When nothing else came, she shrugged. "They're not big on talk, are they?"

"Nope, they sure aren't." Tasha laughed. "But they are as loyal as the day is long."

Sophia frowned at that. "Maybe … but only if you actually get accepted into that inner group."

"It's not about any inner groups. It's about being one with them," she stated. "You've already got an in with them."

"Not likely," she muttered. "I forced my way into this, when you think about it from their perspective."

"Wade let you stay, didn't he?" Tasha asked, with a smirk. "Nobody is forcing Wade to do that. Totally his call. And believe me. If Terk or Damon didn't want you here, you wouldn't be."

"Interesting," Sophia murmured, as she looked at her

friend. "Do you have a say in any of this?"

"It depends on the topic of course, so not a whole lot in a tactical sense, but, if I feel strongly about something, you can bet I speak up," Tasha stated. "I've been part of the team long enough that, when things don't feel right, you can bet I squawk."

At that, Sophia burst out laughing. "*Squawk*, huh?"

"Yeah, nice terminology, I know." She grinned. "But you can't really say anything about what's going on here until you've been here for a while, until you understand more about how the team operates," she stated, "and some of it can be pretty rough."

"I believe you," Sophia agreed. "It seems like a lot of this can be pretty rough."

"Absolutely, but we're getting there, and, as soon as we get this bullshit done with," she stated, with a confidence that she obviously believed, "I'm sure they'll set up shop again, one way or another."

"And you'll stay with them."

"I go wherever the hell Damon goes," she stated, looking over at her friend. "For me that's nonnegotiable."

Sophia nodded. "Well, if I was on better footing with Wade, I might say the same," she agreed. "At the moment it just feels very much like I'm on sufferance."

"Then you have to make sure that sufferance becomes a whole lot more," Tasha replied.

"And I'd like to. I really would. I just don't know how to make that happen, especially under these circumstances."

Tasha smiled at her. "You'll find a way."

And, with that, Sophia headed back to her computer. "I don't even know what I'm supposed to be doing."

"Your job right now and your only job," Tasha stated

firmly, "is to track our guys and to let me know if anything happens."

It wasn't what Sophia was used to, and the inactivity was definitely not her usual thing, but she could get behind this. As Tasha looked on, Sophia brought the satellite feed up close, zooming in on the location. "That helps a lot," she muttered.

Tasha leaned over. "Yeah, that's much clearer. What did you do?"

As Sophia explained the adjustments she made, the two men split up. "Oh, no, no, no, don't do that," she cried out to the empty screen.

"Yep, like I said, it's your job. Looks like now you've got two of them to track separately."

"Shit. That's not cool."

"Cool or not, that's the deal because these guys will be heading off, looking at two different targets, so they'll split up, and what we have to do is make sure that they both get back home again."

Groaning at that, Sophia sat back down and watched. She thought she could tell which one was Damon and could separate out Wade. They were different heights, different densities. And that seemed like kind of a foolish way to describe it, but it was how it felt.

As the men moved forward, she watched, and then they went into the building, and she wished she could do something with that. Now all they could do was wait to see who came out. And that wouldn't tell her jack, until there was actually a problem. She tried to search for a network that she could hack into to access cameras around the location. The halfway house was a low-rent, pay-as-you-stay place, so probably not much of anything high-tech to access, and that would be worse for the guys. They were going in blind.

Surprised, Sophia did find a security system, which she quickly hacked into and brought up the feed. Two men walked through the second floor hallway. "Well, they split up for a minute," she noted, "but they're back together again now."

"Interesting." Tasha glanced over her shoulder. "Oh, good, you got into the security feed. Nice work."

"Yeah, I did," she replied. "Now it looks like they're heading for one room. Is it possible these guys are sharing?"

"Absolutely, wouldn't you?"

"Only one reason why they would share one room, so they probably don't have money," she noted. "I hadn't considered that, but it is a viable point."

As soon as Damon and Wade reached the door, Sophia tuned the picture a little more, checking out and writing down time stamps at crucial points. When the door opened, one of the young men stepped out. She immediately sent a text to Wade. **That was the one who talked the most.** "They shouldn't be going in there," Sophia stated.

"You can't stop this," Tasha replied. "You just have to watch and to trust them to do their job."

"Oh, I trust them. I just don't trust the rest of the world that seems to have absolutely no regard for their well-being."

"That's our job." Tasha pointed to the monitors.

And, of course, Wade's vitals were still calm and steady. Sophia groaned. "I'd really rather be out there with him."

"Yeah, I hear you, but, right now, as shorthanded as we are, we need you here."

"You could do this without me," she argued.

"I could, but, at the moment, I also have to track all these." Tasha nodded at her multiple monitors.

Sophia frowned. "What's all that?"

"It's the feeds from the rest of our team," she explained. "Whenever Terk needs to go down—as in, really power down—he has to shut off his internal surveillance systems. It's the only way he can really recharge at this level. But, when there's a need to keep an eye on the others, he sets up this surveillance for me to use."

"Are we expecting more attacks?"

Tasha just looked at her.

"Okay, stupid question, sorry. Why is that one so much livelier?" she asked, pointing to one particular section of Tasha's nearest screen.

"That's Gage. He's coming out of the coma. I have to watch him carefully because, when he regains consciousness, I'll need to alert Terk quickly, since Gage is likely to be pretty upset, disoriented, and unable to figure out what the hell happened to his life," she stated. "So that's bad news."

"Got it," Sophia replied, "but wow, I'm seeing a lot of movement there."

"Yeah," Tasha agreed. "It's just not necessarily the movement that we need yet." And, with that, she wouldn't say anything more.

Sophia figured it would be one mystery after another, until she either proved herself or until they decided that it was worth telling her all the ins and outs of whatever the hell was going on. Really this was all about trust, which in a way was understandable, since they had been so horribly betrayed.

She got that, and, as she turned to look back at Damon and Wade on her monitor, she wished they all trusted her more. But it would be a process. Frustrated, she settled back to watch the screen.

WADE STEPPED FORWARD and introduced himself to the second guy, who sat in front of a gaming system. "I hear you had a meeting with an older woman today."

The young man looked at him blankly. "Who the hell are you, and what are you doing here?" he asked. The guy they'd shouldered inside the room from the doorway was still rubbing his arm.

"Well, we can keep playing games if you want, but you harassed somebody I know about the groceries she bought," he explained, and, at that, the two young men stiffened. Wade nodded. "Yeah, and you should be scared right now. I'm surprised you're even alive."

"Why the hell wouldn't we be?" the belligerent one snapped.

"Well, did you get any information to tell the guy who paid you?"

"I have no idea what you're talking about," he replied a bit nervously.

"Yeah, you didn't have enough information to make him happy, I'll bet. When are you supposed to go out again?"

"What are you talking about?" he asked. "Man, you're just like the rest of this bloody place. You've lost it."

"I disagree," Wade replied. "You guys won't be delivering any more information."

"Sure we are," he retorted, "and you sure as hell can't stop us." He looked over at Damon, smiled. "You guys are pretty smug, and you probably think your shit doesn't stink in the night."

Damon replied, "I'm pretty damn sure I don't give a fuck, but hassling women over groceries, now that's just bad news. Who put you up to it?"

"What? Was the old gal your girlfriend?" he asked with a snigger. "We just wanted to scare her a little. Life gets boring when you've got nothing to do but play games."

"Yeah, so you hook up with these guys to get paid for hassling folks, huh?"

At that, the young man turned and glared at him, "You don't know jack shit."

"I know more than you know," Damon stated, "and the fact that you're still alive means either they haven't got around to killing you yet or they still have another use for you."

"Of course we're useful," he blustered. "Jesus, it's not like we're just flies to be swatted dead when we're on our way."

But looking at him and wondering what drugs these guys were on, Wade nodded. "But you are. I don't give you even twenty-four hours to live." He looked at Damon. "It's really sad."

"Well, the gunmen *are* cleaning up the streets." Damon shrugged. "I don't feel any particular sadness at losing these two."

"What are you talking about, *losing* us?"

"Don't worry about it," the quieter one stated, trying to soothe the talkative one. "They're just trying to scare us."

But Damon and Wade saw that they were both a little unnerved.

"It doesn't matter, does it though? Because you guys got this," Damon repeated, with a snide smile.

The kid nodded slowly. "Absolutely we do. What the hell are you going on about anyway?"

"These guys who hired you two are professional killers,"

Wade explained.

The one guy puffed up, as if he was thrilled to be part of such an elite group.

At that, Damon just shook his head. "You really don't get it, do you? Don't you realize that you're disposable and that the minute they are done with you, you'll be taken out very quickly."

"Like hell," the one spat, still puffed up. "Do you think we don't know our own value?"

Damon sighed. "I'm pretty sure you don't," he muttered. "And it doesn't matter because now—as soon as we found you, as soon as we walked in here—it's all about somebody else taking you out before you've even had a chance to live, but whatever." Damon shrugged, then turned as if to go.

"No way they'd take us out," the quiet one replied, looking puzzled. "Why would they? We're just doing a couple odd jobs for them."

The other one chimed in. "Okay, so hassling that woman was weird. We were just sitting here, when they called us out of the blue."

"Hey, hey, hey, you shouldn't be talking to them." The quiet one was now panicking.

"Maybe not," he replied, "but we didn't do anything wrong. I mean, nothing really wrong. Like what the hell? What's he doing, talking about us being taken out?"

"Calm down. They're just trying to scare us!"

"Well, they succeeded. I mean, I didn't do anything, so why the hell should anybody be talking about killing us?"

The quiet one glared at his buddy. "You said it would just be easy money."

"Well, it was pretty easy money, wasn't it?"

"Yeah, so far. As long as that's all it is," he replied, "but, if they come back, wanting more from us, it won't be as easy. You know that."

"Well, so far it's been pretty damn fine, so what do we care?"

"Well, you should care," Damon interjected, "because these guys don't fool around."

"Of course they don't. They're pros." The guy was now in full-on talkative mode. "They made it clear that we'd be part of the big leagues."

"No, no, no. I didn't hear anything about being part of the big leagues," the second one argued. "You said we would just earn a little cash. Hell, I don't want any part of this."

"No, maybe not, because you are content just sitting around playing games. You were up for hassling people. It was just for a bit of a lark."

"Sure, as long as that's all we were doing, but not if it'll be anything more serious," he argued, staring at his friend. "What the hell kind of shit have you got us into anyway?" he muttered.

The puffed-up one shrugged. "Nothing serious. It's nothing, so stop panicking."

"*Stop panicking*. Right," he snapped. "The last time somebody told me that was when we were doing a drug that he'd stolen from God-only-knows where." He shook his head. "And believe me. I should have panicked then because that was one hellish trip that I didn't ever really recover from." He raised his right hand. "I haven't touched drugs since."

"Well, it sounds like it might have been a good thing then." Damon looked at him carefully. "Listen. These guys are bad news."

He nodded slowly. "So, it's starting to sound that way, and that doesn't make me happy at all." He got up and walked over to the door. "You know what? It's been fun, but, if you're hooking up into this shit, I'm out of here."

The trouble was, the scared young man didn't realize that there was no getting out of this and that the sadness was about to start. "You do realize you don't get to walk now, right? We would like to see you guys walk away and get the hell out of this"—Wade shrugged—"but they won't let you."

"When you said they were pros, what kind of pros did you mean?" the one guy asked his buddy.

"The big leagues, man. I told you, big leagues."

Damon was looking at him, shaking his head. "Think contract killers."

The puffed-up one sank down onto the couch.

"Holy shit, dude." The kid at the door looked over at his friend. "If you've gotten us into that kind of a shithole, we're in deep trouble."

"Well, I'm staying. I haven't had this kind of money in forever." He looked at Wade and Damon defiantly. "And you can't fucking stop me."

"We don't have to," Wade replied, sadness in his voice. "Because they won't let you live anyway." At that, the other kid bolted out the door.

Damon turned to Wade. "How long do you think they'll give him?"

"Five minutes."

"What are you talking about?" the defiant young man asked, racing to the window. "He's fine. Look at him. He's just fine."

Wade walked to the window to look out himself. Even as he watched, the kid ran for a truck on the far side of the parking lot. He almost made it. His hand was outstretched for the door, with an expression of relief on his face. Then a buzz sounded, and his head split open.

Beside Wade, the defiant kid started to panic and screamed. "Oh my God. Oh my God. They killed him, man. They killed Danny. Oh my God, now they'll kill me."

Damon waved his arm in front of him, trying to get his attention.

"Holy fuck, holy fuck, what did they do?" he asked. "Why did they do that?"

"We told you. They always tie up the loose ends," Damon explained. "They're getting rid of anybody involved. They intentionally choose young kids, punk kids, who think that they can make big money, easy money."

"But we just were hassling people. All we did was follow her."

"And then you took off, right?" Wade asked.

"Yeah, because this guy was taking pictures of us." He indicated Damon.

"The minute he took pictures of you, and you told your new friends, you signed your own death warrant," Wade stated. "Now do you want to tell us who these guys are?" But the kid was too panicked. Wade grabbed him by the arm, sat him back down on the couch. "Start talking. We need to know who these assholes are."

"You're the ones who told us about them." He stared at Wade and Damon. "How do you not even know who they are?"

"We've seen their type before, and we've been following them. We know what they're up to, but we need to know how to get a hold of them."

"I don't know how to get a hold of them."

"Well, how did they get a hold of you then?" Wade asked in exasperation.

The kid held out his phone. "They texted me."

"What? They just texted you out of the blue? How did they find you? When did you first meet?"

He shook his head. "We were just out walking." He flushed. "Okay, so we were drinking heavily off to the side street over there, and this guy approached us," he stated. "He asked if we wanted to make some easy money."

"And of course you said yes," Wade noted.

"Right." He looked at Wade. "You know that it's hard to make ends meet sometimes."

"You could try getting a job," Damon suggested. The guy glared at him, as Damon continued. "So, then you gave him your phone number and agreed?"

He nodded. "They just called us out of the blue and said they had a woman on a nearby street, who we were supposed to hassle." He was recovering somewhat and calming down. "We were supposed to follow her all the way to her place and figure out where she lived, but then, when you started taking photos of us, we backed off."

"And they probably didn't like that you backed off. Is that the deal?"

"He didn't sound very happy about it, but, at the same time, he didn't seem like he was superpissed about it either." He shrugged. "I don't know what the big deal was. I mean, they knew roughly where she lived anyway. I don't know. She wasn't young or terribly pretty, if they were looking to do a midnight raid or something. Jesus! There would have been a lot of other people around they could have taken."

"Maybe," Wade replied, his voice hard. "Go on."

"I mean, we told them what we knew, and they told us

to go home, and, when they had another job, they'd contact us."

"And how did you get the money?"

"It was in the doorjamb," he replied. "I thought that was kind of cool, like supersecret spy stuff." Then he remembered his friend out in the parking lot, as even now people were gathered around and sirens could be heard in the distance. "God, they didn't have to kill him," he whined. "And how did they do it? I didn't see anybody out there."

"They used a drone," Wade stated. "So you were right about supersecret spy stuff, but, unfortunately for your buddy, he's seen the last of it."

"Jesus," he said, "you got to help me. How do I get out of this?"

"I don't know," Wade admitted. "You might want to tell the cops what you know, when they come here asking."

"The cops? No, no, no, no. You don't understand"—he waved his arms about—"I've already got a record, and I can't afford to go back inside. That'll be complete shit for me."

"Well, maybe you should have thought of that before you started doing things like this," Wade noted in exasperation. "Besides, if you're in jail, maybe the killers won't hurt you."

"No, if they've got superspy stuff," he repeated, "they'll take me out right away, won't they?" His bottom lip trembled. "Jesus Christ, what have I done?" He looked at the two men. "But if you guys are here when the cops come, it'll be you who has to answer all those questions." He seemed relieved. "And I can get the hell out of here." He looked out the window again. "A big crowd's out there." Without warning, he just booked it, flat-out racing for the front door and across to the stairs.

Damon and Wade exchanged glances. "You want to go after him?"

"Not particularly. Besides, all we'll be doing is delaying the inevitable."

"Ouch," Damon replied.

Wade nodded. "Don't forget. They went after Sophia."

"At least they didn't hurt her," Damon reminded him. "Cops are down there now. Maybe we should give them a heads-up."

Just then Wade's phone rang. He answered it.

"I got it," Sophia said in lieu of a greeting.

"Got what?" he muttered.

"I got tracking on the drone."

He stiffened and glanced over at Damon. "You actually got a lock on the drone?"

"Yeah, I'm locking in now."

"Jesus, a kid's about to get shot. If you can do something, stop it."

"I'll see," she replied, but her voice was distant. Wade heard her tapping her keys like crazy.

Damon raced over. "Can she really do that?"

"She's trying," he told Damon. To Sophia, he stated, "And, if there's any way to do it on a subtle basis, so they don't really know what happened to the drone, that would be even better. Because we would really like to get a hold of the assholes who are operating this thing. They killed one of the guys who hassled you, and we're pretty sure the other one's the next to go."

"I'm sure he is, if they already took out one." Her voice remained distant, and Wade could tell that he was distracting her, so he pinched his lips together and waited.

"Okay, I just lowered the charge on it. It shouldn't fire,

and they may not have any idea what happened."

"What's it doing now?"

"It's heading back. It's going home. I'm still tracking it."

They looked at each other, smiled.

"Still, I'm not sure it was worth saving that kid's life. Who knows what other crimes he'll graduate to."

"Maybe not," Wade replied gently. "But sometimes we have to do the right thing, even when they don't deserve it."

She laughed. "Well, now that you don't have those punks to talk to, you want to come on home, so I don't have to sit here and worry about you?" And, with that, she hung up.

"Is that all she's doing? Worrying about me?" Wade slowly put away his phone.

"Absolutely," Damon agreed. "If you're beside her, she's keeping track of what you say and do to make sure that it's all good, and, if you're not beside her, she's constantly pivoting to look at the door to make sure you haven't opened it and stepped out."

Wade frowned. "She's got to learn to trust."

"She doesn't know what she has to trust in yet, and, until you fill her in on all this, it'll be hard for her. But believe me. So far she's a trooper, and she has already proven to be a valuable asset to the team, time and time again."

"I told you that she was good."

"Yeah, so how come we didn't bring her onto the team a while ago?"

"I can only tell you what Terk told me. He'd actually considered it apparently, but, because you and Tasha were still working things out"—Damon added an eye roll—"Terk didn't want to complicate things further by adding Sophia into the mix." Wade frowned at Damon, considering these last words of his. "And what happened this time to change Terk's mind?"

"He did it because of where Sophia's coming from," Damon admitted.

"And where's that?" Wade asked, bewildered.

Damon didn't hold back. "From the heart, man. According to Terk, she loves you—and not just a little bit but a lot. And, if you don't feel the same way, that's a hard burden," Damon replied, his voice dropping into low tones. "How do you feel?"

"Oh, I love her a lot," Wade stated. "The hardest thing I ever did was walk away, but I thought I needed to do that for her sake."

"You do know that women really hate it when you say that, right?"

"Yeah, she has told me that a time or two. We obviously still have some things to shake out, but, well, maybe there's a chance for us after all." Wade looked over at his buddy. "Who would have thought that, through this whole nightmare, we'd find partners, after all these years of deliberately keeping ourselves away from all that."

"And the reason we did is because of shit like this." Damon shook his head. "I don't know if I'll ever sleep again worrying about Tasha, but she's a trooper too. She has always been there for me, so it's pretty hard for me to walk away and to tell her to go."

"You don't want to anyway, do you?"

"Hell no," he snapped. "Of course I don't. But sometimes you wonder if you even have choices anymore. All this shit coming down is happening so fast, and people are pulling our strings. That makes you angry, and you want to yank back."

"Hell," Wade replied. "I'm beyond angry, and I think it's well past the point in time that we start doing the yanking. We're still playing catch up with these guys. They're getting out ahead of us, and we're just reacting. Seriously we need to get ahead of them for a change."

"Got it." Damon looked at him and asked, "Are you ready to go back?"

"Hell yeah. Time for plan B. Maybe by then we'll have a location for that damn drone. I'd like to stop whoever's on the other end of that thing and have a visit with him."

"Well, he's the one target we're after right now," Damon agreed. "So let's go get him."

CHAPTER 11

S OPHIA WORKED AWAY on the computer. "Come on, you little bugger." She ferociously tracked the drone's signal back to its source. Tasha stood behind her, watching the screen. Terk was by her side, fresh out of his recharging session.

"How close are you?" Tasha asked, walking closer to Sophia's screen. And then she stopped. "Oh my God, you're almost there."

"I am." When the tracker in front of her started to pulse, she made a crowing sound. "And we got it. Yes!"

"What exactly did we get though?" Terk asked, still staring at the screen.

"We got the drone, and now we have the drone's location."

He looked at her with interest. "As in a physical address?"

"In a few seconds, yes." Just as coordinates popped onto the screen in front of her, it quickly converted to a street address. "There you go"—she pointed—"a physical address."

He stared at the location on the map. "That's not very far from here, in outer Manchester."

"No, none of this has been very far from here," she noted. "It seems like basically they've been playing with us the whole damn time."

"Well, that's about to come to an end," Terk muttered. Then he stepped off to the side, presumably to contact the others.

Sophia looked over at Tasha, a big grin on her face. "Okay, what's next?" she asked, still on the high of success. "Who else can we track down?"

"Anybody and everyone," Tasha stated immediately. "But first, see if we can get any information on that address."

"I'm on it." Sophia's fingers moved quickly over her keyboard.

"Like, who owns it, who is in residence, et cetera. The deeds and any history associated with that. Bank records of any names associated with it. Anything. You never know what could help." Tasha shook her head.

Sophia grinned, waggling her eyebrows. "I do love tracking personal shit. People always think they are so smart when they try to hide their tracks."

Beside her, Tasha started to laugh. "You are a born hacker, girl."

"Oh, and like you aren't." Sophia looked over at her friend and laughed.

"Well, sometimes I forget what it's like." Tasha nodded. "The chase, the thrill of the slightly unethical aspect."

"Well, this is ethical," Sophia stated. "We're under attack. That makes it war, and, in war, anything goes. Particularly when it comes to them killing people in the streets."

"Right," Tasha agreed. "I get these guys pissed somebody off, but wow. Seriously I don't even know what they could have done that was worth being killed over. It sounds like they were pretty arrogant to you but not necessarily that bad."

"No, not at all, and Damon chased them off," she stated. "The minute he drove up, taking pictures of them, they freaked in a quiet way and disappeared."

"It's bound to all make sense later. We're just missing the rest of the pieces to see the big picture. But we'll be filling that in right now," Tasha noted, as she watched Sophia moving her fingers quickly over the keyboard surface.

"Okay," Sophia replied. "I've got the drone house in outer Manchester. It's registered to a Poma. William Poma." She moved the screen with the name off to the side. "He's, well, look at that, another IT engineer." Sophia then started to swear. "What do you want to bet he's already dead?"

"I'm not betting anymore in this case," Tasha noted, "because it seems like people are being taken out so fast that we have no shot at getting ahead of it."

"And that's about to change," Terk stated. "The guys were on their way back, but I've sent them over to this Poma address instead."

Tasha nodded. "They should get there in no time. What about your brother? Are you sending him there too?"

"Talking to him now." Terk held his phone to his ear, not wasting any time.

"Right, we're a little short on men."

"We are," Terk agreed, "but we've been short on men before."

Sophia nodded and didn't say anything. It was almost standard when it came to the espionage world. If it wasn't a shortage of able-bodied men, it was a shortage of men you could trust. And that was just a hell that knew no end. She immediately brought up all the information she had found so far, including financials, work history, tickets, and criminal record. "Oh, look. I've got two William Pomas, both at the same address. But not junior and senior. Maybe granddad and grandson? Anyway, the younger William Poma got a DUI four years ago and lost his job at the same time. Looks like he's been on a downturn ever since, until about six months ago when money started to pile up in his bank account again. Before that, it had been pretty slim pickings for a while," she muttered, as she continued looking back a few years at the balances month to month. "So whatever it was that happened in his world six months ago, it brought him a bonanza of cash."

"Yeah, but you have to live to spend it," Tasha pointed out.

"True enough," Sophia muttered, "but I don't think these guys ever think about that."

"That's because they think they're on the winning side. They don't consider the fact that, one of these days, they won't be needed anymore. Or they think that they'll get out fast enough that it won't be an issue." She shook her head. "Still, it's sad to see so many otherwise good people going down the tube like this."

"It is. It is, indeed." It didn't take long before Sophia had done a full sweep on the property details. "I've got the satellite picking up that property as well," Tasha noted. "It just finally connected, and we'll have a picture in three … two … one … and there." She pointed to a screen, off to one side.

Terk walked over to take a look. "Looks like another one of those old-style mansions on a bit of acreage a little out of town, private."

"I wonder if they're targeting these properties."

"Not likely, yet a lot of these are around England. Only since this trend to modernize every single thing has it become popular to target and to tear down these older places."

"I really like them." Sophia studied the stately mansion. "It's pretty sad when we start taking all the old architecture that has meaning and throwing it to the ground." She felt sad as she looked at it. "Decades of history are in these places."

"Very true," Terk agreed, "but that doesn't really help our people now."

"Nope, it sure doesn't," Sophia muttered. She checked some of the other documents she had found. "Looks like elder Poma does work from home. I bet grandson William Poma lives in the basement, playing video games. I have no idea if anybody has been around or seen either of them recently."

"Cameras. There are street cameras," Tasha said suddenly. And she logged into the traffic system.

So did Sophia. "Tell me what cam you have, and I'll take the other."

Tasha continued. "There is one at the intersection for sure, probably another on the other intersection." With that, she went back a week, then started fast-forwarding and marking down the vehicles that approached the house.

"I have three vehicles approaching the house within seven days," Sophia noted. "One stayed for about two hours. Another was there for several hours and could have been the one that belongs there." She paused. "It's pretty hard to tell at this point, but it left for a few hours and came back again."

"So there's a good possibility that it may be one of the William Pomas who belong there," Terk replied.

"It's possible," Sophia replied, "but then this car came."

And she brought up another vehicle.

Instantly Tasha smiled. "That's the one we're after," she noted. "Nice find, Sophia."

"Why that one?" Terk asked.

Tasha smiled. "We saw that vehicle at the second Liverpool house—where hacker Randall Godwin was squatting—but parked a little farther away. Our enemies are using their own drones to track and kill their own IT guys—or the two street thugs. Wow."

Then Sophia pulled up some later camera feeds, looking for the one vehicle she was after, and added, "This is it." And there it was, the same vehicle from Liverpool, now parked outside the Poma estate in outer Manchester. "Now what we don't have is anything on the actual driver," she noted in frustration. "Nothing is close enough to actually see who it even is. We don't even know for sure if it's a guy, do we?" she asked, suddenly looking over at Tasha.

"Nope, short of our guys finding a person on the ground, we don't have that kind of digital intel yet," Tasha murmured. "Unless you can find something that points us in one way or the other."

"No luck so far." Sophia switched screens. She flexed her fingers and got down to work again.

Behind her, Terk suggested, "Look. If you need a break—"

"No time for that." Sophia brushed him off. "But thank you for thinking of it."

He frowned. "You know that there's no point in taking down these guys if we get overtired to the point of wearing ourselves out or getting someone hurt in the process."

"Exactly. That's why I'm not stopping yet." Sophia wouldn't give Terk the chance to get on her nerves. "The last thing we want is our guys getting hurt."

She felt the two of them exchanging glances behind her back. "Look. I get it. We need to do this, and we also need to do it with some semblance of control, which is why I'm at it still," she explained. "Information is the highway to power, and, if we don't have any intel, we won't get anywhere." She now brought up multiple screens.

"What's this?" Terk asked, pointing at one of Sophia's new screens.

"A list of known associates from when the younger William Poma guy spent time in jail with his DUI. It's cross-referencing against his neighbors, against the owners of the vehicles that approached and disappeared from this same property, and known associates from his line of work. Looks like we've got two names coming up." Sophia brought them up on the screen. "We've got a Thomas Delaware, and a ... oh look at this, Jamison Delaware. Brothers from the looks of it."

"Could be father and son," Terk added.

"True enough." Sophia nodded. "I need to keep digging to find out more." It didn't take but a matter of minutes for her to bring them up in living color. "Looks like the brothers Delaware, and a rough-looking lot they are." She pointed them out for Terk. Then she went on looking into their records and their financials. "Same thing. We've got an increase in their finances coming into play about six months ago." She brought up their bank accounts, then their court documents. "And we have two counts of forgeries for each of them. They got off pretty lightly as first-time offenders, and, in both cases, they were juveniles. Well, not quite juvenile, I guess. They were nineteen and already heading down the wrong track. Looks like they didn't get enough of a deterrent and kept on going," she muttered.

"And it happens. As we know, it really does," Terk agreed.

"I just think it's too bad when people are given a chance, and they don't put it to good use."

He smiled. "That's because you want to see people do something good with their life."

"Well, it would sure be nice if they did," Sophia muttered. "Instead of joining the ranks of the assholes of the world."

He laughed. "That's one way to put it, but there will always be assholes though."

"And what if we're a little tired of assholes?" Sophia shot him a look.

"Well, the fact of the matter is, plenty of them are in our world, and that's why we're out here. Nobody curtailed these guys or dealt with the people behind the scenes, all building them into the problem people they are now," he replied.

"You mean, the ones in their past, their family, friends, who gave them money and free reign to terrorize people?" Sophia asked.

He nodded.

"Which is why we do what we do. I got it," she murmured. "I've sent a text with the Delaware brothers' photos and names to Wade."

He just smiled at her as she kept on going, her keyboard clattering.

"Something moving on the screen," Tasha said, from beside Sophia, where Tasha had been monitoring the satellite image. "We've got activity at the address."

Sophia stopped and moved over to see what Tasha was looking at.

"Okay," Tasha noted, "it's Damon and Wade. What do you suppose they'll find?"

"With our luck, another body," Sophia muttered.

"I hope not," Tasha replied in a dark tone.

"I'll send them a quick text on the two William Poma guys who live there. And attach their photos too. Just in case."

Tasha shook her head. "I mean, at some point in time, the bad guys'll run out of people to kill."

"Nope. Nearing eight billion people on this planet. The killer will find a victim no matter what."

Tasha looked over at her friend. "Since when did you become so negative?"

"Yeah, when I started working in this field," Sophia replied. "Hacking became pursuing predators, and, fun or not fun, it's a necessity." She shook her head. "Unfortunately there always seems to be another predator, and that is something I just don't get. Like how can there be so many assholes in this world?"

"What was it you just said about almost eight billion people on this planet?" Terk asked.

She nodded. "Agreed, there are that many, but how come so many of them are just assholes?"

"Because they're trying to crawl their way on top of the good people to get where they want to be," Tasha replied. "They don't care about helping anybody else. Selfish assholes. They just want what they want and don't care who they have to take out to get it."

"Like I said, assholes," Sophia muttered, her keys still clattering, as she pulled up information. "We've got schools, educational records, and known associates. And now we've got two more pings because they have somebody in common." She skittered through the information. "Who is that?" she muttered, and then she crowed. "Here you go. The dead body found at the last place in Liverpool—Randall Godwin—was friends with this younger William Poma guy too."

"So, chances are, Poma probably got Randall or even Rodney into the deal or vice versa."

"That makes sense."

Tasha called their attention back to the satellite screen, and they watched as Wade and Damon spread out and headed toward the front door of the drone operator, Poma's, estate. When they knocked on the front door, and no sound came from inside, the guys split up, but both ended up at the rear door.

Sophia watched, feeling her throat tighten up. "It's really unnerving watching these guys work in real time. It's like a bad movie that you keep hoping will have a different ending, but you're afraid it'll be the same damn thing all over again."

"As long as the different ending doesn't mean that they get hurt," Tasha noted beside her.

"God no, please not," Sophia whispered.

Tasha looked over and squeezed her shoulder. "Wade is a pro, and he really does know what he's doing."

"He does. I know. And my reaction is not a reflection on my belief in his abilities, not at all," Sophia stated. "But it sure is frustrating when I know he's not operating at full power, you know, in whatever way you want to utilize that," she murmured.

"Hey, that's not a bad way of putting it." Tasha laughed. "You're getting good at that."

"No, I'm not," she argued. "I'm trying to pick up the jargon as I go along, but I'm telling you. It's not easy."

"None of this stuff is easy," Tasha agreed, with a smile,

"but that doesn't mean it's not worthwhile."

"Agreed ... totally agreed." Sophia nodded. "It's just, you know, hard." And, with that, she turned back and watched as Wade looked at his phone, probably reading her texts, then the two men disappeared inside the house.

STANDING JUST INSIDE the kitchen door, Wade sent out an energy probe. Outside they hadn't discerned much, but he was still looking for the signature of whoever had attacked them before. As he sent out another probe, he froze and looked over at Damon, then held out a hand and put up two fingers. Damon's eyebrows shot up. In a low voice, Wade whispered, "One is a signature who already attacked us."

At that, Damon's face locked down hard. Wade nodded, and, exchanging some hand motions, they split up. As Damon circled to the left, Wade went right and headed through the kitchen, then the dining room, looking for anything that would show them where these two guys were.

It was all BS as far as Wade was concerned. These guys shouldn't get away with this crap, but it looked like it was that much harder to do anything about it when their opponents had so much advanced tech equipment— hardware and software—plus endless cheap lackeys available to them. Not to mention Terk's team was only partially available at the moment and also was completely on their own for the first time, without the US government's assistance in any form.

Wade calculated the losses to their team, while cloaking himself, desperately trying not to give away his own location, what with his energy drain happening. Only so much he could do.

Every once in a while, he'd get wind of some different energy surge coming his way, and he took advantage of those. He didn't know the source of this energy or why it was coming to him at all, but he wouldn't argue with accepting it. He needed it too damn much and could use a little more of it too.

Almost instantly more of it was available, seemingly pouring his way. He frowned, trying to understand this power source, but he couldn't take his focus off what was happening around him. *Later*, he promised himself. After this was over, he'd figure out what the hell was going on. In the meantime, he had other things to deal with, and that was frustrating too. As he swept through the lower part of the house, he met Damon on the other side. Both shook their heads, and they headed up the stairs.

The steps creaked, which was yet another concern. But they were good at this, and Wade wasn't about to let it stop him. As soon as they cleared the stairs, they moved through the second floor, seeing just what was going on here. But again, Wade heard nothing, but he found a dead body stashed in a crawl space access along the hallway. It matched one of the photos Sophia had texted him. *Thomas Delaware.* Wade shared that photo with Damon.

With the check of the full upstairs done, Wade and Damon slowly moved downstairs.

As they reached the main floor again, they heard voices coming up from the basement.

"That drone is pretty sweet, isn't it?"

"Well, it was ... when it worked," the other voice snapped. "We really can't afford to have it not work some of the time. That failure caused us major trouble."

"Yeah, I think it was just not holding the charge or something. I'll change out the battery, although it is nearly brand new."

"I don't care if it's brand new or not," the other voice barked. "We can't take a chance."

"Nope, I got it. And I can track this guy, the next time he pops his head out anywhere," he stated. "Then we'll take him down."

"You better," he noted.

"Hey, no problem ... Just relax."

But there was no relaxing for the other man. This poor guy just didn't know it.

Wade wondered if the drone operator would be taken out right now or if the other man would wait until the drone was fixed and had done its job. But Wade knew these guys operated in their own completely amoral lifestyle. They would do whatever the hell they wanted to do, and it didn't matter one bit what anybody else said.

Wade and Damon waited until the guys left the basement and walked into the kitchen, then surprised them from behind.

"Hands up," they both snapped.

The two men froze and then slowly turned around, their hands in the air.

The one guy, the naïve one, soon-to-be-killed Poma, looked at Wade in complete shock.

"What the hell is going on here?" he asked. "How dare you come into my house like this," he yelled in outrage.

Wade chuckled. "Not your house though, legally. It's Grandpa's, isn't it?" When the kid clammed up, Wade continued. "Where is Grandpa?"

"On holiday."

"I hope so, kid."

The kid frowned. "I'll call the cops."

"Well, that would be a good thing," Damon agreed, with a laugh, "but I highly doubt you really want the cops around."

Poma froze. "What the hell do you mean?"

"You think we don't know the killing drone came from here?" Damon asked. "Do you think that your upset associate here isn't trying to figure out if you messed things up with the drone somewhere along the line and if it's your fault that the second street thug kid *isn't* dead yet?" One shock after another hit the expressions of the two men, who realized just how much Wade and Damon knew.

"Who are you?" the second guy asked, his voice dark, threatening.

Wade nodded. Telepathically to Damon, he said, *Yeah, this was the familiar signature Somehow this guy has attacked us before. If not involved with the original takedown of our team with the special interference software, then this guy had been involved since then, most likely with the drones. Possibly both.* Wade smiled. "Nobody you need to concern yourself with," Wade replied in a hard tone. "I presume you killed the two Godwin brothers, your own IT guys, we found at the two houses in Liverpool." At that, Wade watched the bully, who was getting paler by the second. He pointed at Poma. "And had this guy shoot the first kid, but he missed the second street thug, didn't he?"

The bully narrowed his eyes.

Wade nodded. "You didn't think you were hiring the best help out there, did you? Really? You know these are just cheap punk-ass hackers and two street thugs, right? They're all about getting money and getting into part of this covert operation bullshit, like in their computer games;, but, when it actually comes down to it, they're all just naïve punks." Wade smiled. "And you." He pointed to Poma, the clueless drone operator. "All these middlemen guys clean up after themselves. Nobody's left alive who's worked for them up until now."

"I don't know what you're talking about," Poma replied nervously, with half a glance sliding to the guy standing at his side, as if waiting for him to refute the claim.

But the mouthy guy just crossed his arms over his chest. "Are you done yet?" he snarled. "This is pretty damn boring."

"Yeah, I imagine it is for you," Wade noted. "I mean, seriously, probably nothing in your world is of interest these days, except your private little vendetta."

"I know who you are," the man said. "And you think that you and your team are hot shit and that nobody comes close, right? Well, I got news for you. Not only will you go down, you'll go down hard."

"Yeah, that's interesting," Damon murmured. "We don't even know why the hell you're after us."

"Oh, you know." He gave a wave of his hand, completely tossing aside Damon's comment. "And, if you don't, you just haven't been paying attention for the last few years."

"Iran," Wade replied, almost out of instinct.

With that, the guy's face hardened yet again, and his gaze narrowed to thin steely pinpoints. "See? Not so hard after all, was it?"

The trouble was, something was off in his voice, and Wade didn't know what the hell that meant either. It was damn frustrating. Getting answers was one thing, but getting the truth was a completely different story. "Well, you're the ones who hired Poma, the drone dude here. You're the ones associated with the attack on our previous headquarters," Wade noted. "So what's your plan now?"

"Well, if you think we'll talk," he replied, "you're idiots."

"I don't think you're an idiot." Wade smiled. "We'll separate you off, and I bet your little drone operator guy here will sing like a canary."

At that, the guy in charge frowned. "He doesn't have anything to say."

"Yeah, I don't have anything to say," Poma repeated nervously.

"Good." Wade nodded. "You'll be really good at withstanding torture then, right?"

Poma made a squeaking sound.

Wade laughed. "Do you really think that all this black ops stuff doesn't come with its own set of perks?"

"I don't know what you're talking about," the drone operator replied, sounding rattled.

"Well then, you haven't been paying attention either. *Tsk, tsk, tsk.* You can't kill a man without expecting retaliation or punishment of some kind," Wade replied.

"I didn't do anything."

"Did you not just operate the drone that took out a kid? Not to mention another one earlier today?"

He swallowed hard, then looked over at his boss, back at Wade again. "Well, not really."

"*Not really?* That's an interesting way to phrase it. *Not really.* Did you hear that, Damon?"

"I heard it," Damon replied easily. "This kid really doesn't have a clue."

"No, they never do," Wade agreed. "They think it's all

fun and games, until it all turns around, and it's them in the hot seat. Then they immediately claim that they don't know anything. But you knew enough to shoot somebody with a drone. Didn't you, Poma?"

Damon added, "Yeah, not only shoot … but kill. So I suppose that's just another notch in your belt, huh?" Damon asked Poma.

At that, the Poma kid grew a little queasy. "That's not really how I wanted to think of it."

"Yeah, well, too bad about that," Damon stated, "because you know that's what these guys do. It's all about numbers for them. They've got a job to do, and they do it."

Wade looked at the guy in charge. "Did Iran pay you already?"

"Wouldn't you like to know."

"Because, of course, you know that, if they paid you, they'll expect results."

"Everybody wants results all the time," he replied. "I've never failed yet."

"No." Damon shook his head. "I don't imagine you have. Unfortunately you won't give them the results this time."

"Yeah … why not?" He gave Damon an odd look; then he reached up, as if to scratch his ear. Almost immediately a weird sensation filled the room.

"Shut it off," Wade roared immediately.

But the other guy just smiled at him. "Shut it off yourself."

Trying to stay upright, Damon looked at Wade, gasping out, "What is it?"

"It's that interference software we've been talking about," he replied, noting the increasing pain.

Damon tried hard to keep from wincing as he stated, "Shut it down."

"Fat chance," the man replied.

"Well, we just might have to shoot him to do that," Wade noted to Damon.

"On the other hand, we could shoot the kid first," Damon suggested.

"No! No, you don't have to shoot me," the kid whined, as if suddenly realizing this wasn't just posturing anymore.

"Yeah? Then shut down the program now!" Wade felt the pressure rising inside his head, starting to drown out everything else. He struggled to focus. He cocked his gun, pointing it at the kid. "Shut it off."

"I-I don't know what you're talking about," he replied nervously. "I don't … I don't have a clue what he's even doing."

The other guy laughed. "Told you." He sneered. "You guys don't know jack shit."

"Oh, we know a lot," Damon stated, "but, if you won't shut it down, you know what's coming."

The guy's face turned dark, and, when he reached up for his ear again, Damon shot his hand.

"What if I was trying to shut it off?" he shouted, holding his hand against his chest.

"Oh, I've got another solution for that." And Wade stepped forward and, with a hard blow, clobbered the man just above the ear. The guy dropped, out cold, and thankfully the noise and the pain stopped.

CHAPTER 12

SOPHIA ANSWERED WADE'S phone call. "Well, at least you got one," she replied, as soon as she heard the news.

"No, we've got two," he corrected, "but one is a kid."

"The drone operator?"

"Yeah, him."

"Good," she replied. "Are you bringing them back?"

"Actually I was hoping that Merk was there. Is Terk around? I tried calling him but didn't get him."

She turned and looked back at Terk. "Wade has been trying to get a hold of you."

Terk looked up, frowned immediately, and closed his eyes.

She immediately lost Wade on the phone. Hanging up, Sophia shook her head. "It'll take a bit to get used to that."

Tasha grinned from ear to ear. "That's okay. I'm adaptable."

Tasha snickered beside her. "That's my girl."

"So weird. They've got two though. And if Merk's not available ..."

"That's good," Tasha stated, then frowned. "Two live ones to interrogate, but we can't bring them back here, which will be the next problem."

"Oh, I didn't even think of that," Sophia replied. "*Hmm*, if they'll interrogate them, do they need anything from here?"

185

"Not likely," Tasha noted. "Besides, you're not going anywhere."

"I probably should, though," Sophia suggested. "I hate to see Wade out there all alone."

"Damon's with him." Again Tasha grinned broadly.

"Fine. I *am* a field operative. Remember?"

"I keep forgetting that." Tasha turned and looked at Terk, who frowned as he looked at both of them.

Sophia stood, walked over. "I'm perfectly capable of doing a prisoner transfer." She slipped on her shoulder holster, loaded it with her weapon. "Come on. This is ridiculous. What do they need?"

"They'll take the two prisoners to another location," Terk noted.

"So it's better if I go to where they are, so I can track down any electronics."

Terk pulled out his phone, then had a fast and intense discussion, while she packed up one of her laptops. Terk disconnected his call and also packed up a box of electronics he wanted her to take along.

"Fine, is this everything? I've got the address already. What vehicle am I taking?" she asked him. Terk handed her the keys to the truck. "Good enough then. I'll be back soon."

He frowned. "Stop for a minute. I want you to think this through."

"You forget I worked for Levi. Freelance, but still as an operative."

He nodded immediately. "You're right. I do keep forgetting that. Sorry."

"Just don't keep it up." She smiled. And, with that, she turned and headed out, hearing an argument behind her, but she ignored it. She wouldn't take offense because they didn't have any female operatives in their world, and, in her world, it was definitely something she'd been up against time and time again. She tried not to let it piss her off, but sometimes it did get to be wearing.

On the other hand, she wasn't sure that she would handle it any better if she were on the other side of the fence. It's what they were used to, and shaking it up was good for them. She drove carefully, checking to make sure she wasn't being followed by the time she made it to the address. She looked out to see Wade standing there on the front steps, waiting for her.

Thankfully no anger was visible on his face. She hopped out, as he raced over, grabbing one of her two boxes. "Let's get inside, stat."

She followed quickly. "More drones?"

"I think they're all centered here," he replied, "but I don't know for sure, so just a precaution."

She walked in to find two men on the floor, both tied up, one out cold, and another was the drone operator she'd tracked earlier to this location. "Anybody talking yet?" she asked. Wade shook his head. "Well, we'll fix that soon enough."

The kid's eyes widened when he saw her.

"What's the matter?" she asked. "Did you think special ops was just for men?" He flushed and she nodded. "I came here to hack your electronics."

The kid frowned, and then his eyes widened, and he shook his head. "You can't. You can't get into my electronics."

"Why not?" she asked. "It's obvious that we need information, and, if you won't talk, well, that's just where we'll go. Besides, I'm sure you keep all kinds of fun stuff in there.

How much of your porn will I have to endure?"

He flushed bright red.

"Don't worry. I really don't care about your collection." Then she stopped and turned. "Unless there's anything other than straight vanilla porn," she replied, "and then I'll nail your ass to the wall."

He immediately shook his head back and forth.

"Right, well anything you jerk off to is your problem," she muttered, shaking her head. He flushed again. She walked over to Wade. "What have you found for electronics?" Wade just pointed to the laptop off to the side. She nodded, sat down.

The kid told her, "You won't get into it."

"Why? Because I'm a woman?" she asked, turning her head to look at him. "And, by the way, I can get into anything." She got in, hit something immediately, showed him the screen, while she continued to watch him, and his eyes grew wide.

"No, no, no, no."

"Too late. See? Next time you open your mouth, at least give me a bit of a challenge," she muttered.

Beside her, Damon laughed, leaned in to whisper to her, "Merk did say you were hell on wheels."

"Damn right," she muttered. "You guys are just too used to protecting the little women at home."

"Well, maybe. We won't make that mistake again anymore," Wade noted.

"Yeah, you will," she replied. "Because you're all about protecting, aren't you? Isn't that why you didn't come back again?"

He understood her point. "Exactly."

"Trouble is, not everybody wants or needs protecting,"

she spat in a hard tone.

"Got it." He nodded. "And you're right. I'm sorry."

"You should be," she snapped. "I'll forgive you this time. Next time I'll whoop your ass. I haven't had a good workout lately, and frankly I'm due."

"Now that sounds like fun," he teased. "Judo, karate, mixed martial arts ... you name it."

"I've dabbled, but I'm not a pro at any of them," she replied, "but I've found something that works for me and have stuck with it."

"What is it that works for you?" he asked curiously, while the kid stared from one to the other in astonishment.

"Anything that goes at the time." She laughed.

"Ah, I can get behind that too." Wade turned to face the kid. "So what's the matter? You didn't know we were just regular people?"

"I didn't think of it," he admitted, shamefaced. "And they made it sound like you guys were really terrible."

Sophia shook her head. "Yeah, and what about the two you killed? He was just looking to make a few bucks to buy some games. Your boss paid those two street thugs a little money to go hassle me, when I was bringing groceries back home." She smiled. "And when somebody drove up and took their picture, they ran like the kids they were. That's who you shot. Only let me get it right. That's who you *murdered*. But what do you care? It was just a kid, *like you*, trying to make his way through life, *the same as you*, only, as far as you're concerned, he was just garbage, right?"

"I didn't know," he said. "That's not what they told us at all."

"Us?" she asked, looking over at Damon and Wade. "Did you find any more of that *us*?"

"No, that's the first time that particular pronoun has been used, but we'll find out now," Damon stated, as he walked closer to the kid.

The kid immediately cringed. "Look. I'll talk ... I'll talk. I didn't know any of this stuff before," he admitted. "They told us that you were thieves, into blackmail, kidnapping, holding families hostage for money, then killing them after they paid."

"Well, they lied," she snapped. "Those two punks were staying in a dumpy halfway house because they were down on their luck, and they hooked up with these bad guys, as they needed a few bucks. They were playing Xbox when we got there."

His bottom lip trembled. "Jesus, what have I done?"

"You committed murder, and, to make it worse, you did it for hire."

His shoulders sagged. "If I talk, will you go easy on me?"

"Whatever goes easy from our side," Wade replied, then pointed to the guy out cold on the floor, "won't protect you from whatever his bosses will do to you."

"I thought he was the boss," the kid cried out.

"No, he's not. He's just another one of the middlemen lackeys. High enough to be out here busily hiring local people to do these little shit jobs, but I don't think he's very high up the shit ladder."

"So what'll happen now?"

"Let's start with something easy. Are you the only one who can operate the drone?"

He swallowed. "Jesus. I won't even see it coming, will I?"

"Well, isn't that what happened to the kids you murdered?" Damon asked.

He nodded slowly, tears welling up in his eyes. "This is

not how I thought my life would go."

"What did you think? What were you expecting? Never mind. It doesn't matter," Wade replied, while Sophia quickly moved her way through the kid's laptop. She found his porn stash and deleted it, despite what she had said earlier. A kid like this could just go find a ton more anyway.

The kid shook his head. "I was thinking of money," he admitted. "I was trying to buy a new gaming rig, and I needed more parts, you know? Trying to soup it up. And the money they offered just hit the right spot."

"Yeah, a human life is pretty cheap these days." She turned to look at him. "What did you get? Five grand?"

He flushed. "No, not even that much."

"Okay, so those kids' lives really weren't worth anything to you then, were they?"

He swallowed yet again. "You make me sound like I'm some sort of killer," he protested.

She looked at him and asked, "Aren't you?"

"No"—he shook his head—"I didn't mean to get involved in something like this."

"No, you didn't *mean* to," she muttered, "but you did, and, even worse, you followed through on it," she snapped. "So who's your buddy who got into this with you?"

"Thomas Delaware," he replied. "And he knew somebody else who was doing it too, so they got him into it."

She turned to Damon, who shook his head.

"Then he tagged me."

She sighed. "So, where's your buddy Thomas now?" she asked.

"He told me that he would take off for a few days. I think he was getting cold feet," he admitted. "Yeah—"

"He's upstairs, kid … dead," Wade interrupted, as he

stood behind Sophia.

At that, the kid shrieked. "Seriously? What the hell?"

"We told you that these guys won't leave anybody alive, and that includes you." Wade shook his head.

"But we didn't do anything to them," he whined, and his naïveté tore at her heart. "It was just a job."

"You may not have done anything to these gunmen, but you know too much, and your bank accounts probably show payments, evidence of your crimes." She tapped the keys, about to look into his. "You got $4,200 bucks to kill those kids? Wow. All of $4,200."

"Get out of my bank account," he roared. "Leave my money alone."

"You don't have any money, kid. You have pennies," she replied.

"What the hell?"

"You have the ability and the talent to do all kinds of shit, and what are you doing? Taking pennies for taking a couple of lives?" she snapped in disgust.

"Well, it's hard to know where to go and to get work anymore," he replied. "It's a different world out there."

"It sure is," she muttered. "A world where you can hire a killer for $4,200 bucks." At that, there was nothing much the kid could say. She turned to Damon. "Is there anything in particular you want out of this?"

He nodded. "Any other connections. Communications. This other guy here, the one who's out cold, he's not talking."

"Did you check Bioscan to see if we've got any identity on them?"

"We got your coworker running it through the database now."

"Good," she noted, "because we obviously need to ID him first."

"His name is Marshall," the kid replied.

"Marshall what?"

"Riley Marshall," he replied. "And he approached the one guy, who approached my friend Thomas, who approached me."

"Did you have any communication with anybody else in the organization? Names?"

"No, I promise. It was just him."

"And how did you guys communicate?"

"Text messages."

"Where did Riley get yours from?"

"I don't know." Poma shrugged. "I presumed it was my buddy."

"And that's probably true, until he was tortured to get information."

"We talked a few times, and then Thomas stopped calling, so I assumed he'd left. I thought I'd talked to him just a few days ago. We've just been really busy on this project. I was so focused on the drone work that I wasn't really worried about him because I knew he was doing other stuff."

"Yeah, he sure was ... trying to save his life. But that slipped away on him anyway."

"Shit! Stop reminding me!" he shouted. He curled up in a ball. "Man, I don't know what I'll do. If my mom finds out, I—"

"Seriously?" Sophia couldn't believe what she was hearing.

Poma flushed again. "Look. You don't understand. She's really an upstanding person, and she'd be so embarrassed."

"*Embarrassed?* What do you think your buddy Thomas's

mother will think? Or the mother of the street kids you killed?" That thought shut him up yet again. "And here you are living for free with Grandpa with not one worry about what he'll say, *huh*?" She spun around and quickly analyzed Poma's emails. "A couple email threads go back and forth. And we've got the wire transfers into his bank account but not a whole lot else in here." She turned and looked at the kid's gaze and saw a flicker. "Well, something else is in here to see though"—she pointed—"if the look on his face is any judge."

Immediately he glared at her.

"Except he's not feeling so helpful right now."

"You're in my goddamn computer," he yelled.

"Yeah, well, let's see what you're building." And she whistled. "See? This just pisses me off. Somebody like this, with brains and no place to go," she muttered. "Did Grandpa help you with this?" The kid refused to answer. Sophia turned toward Wade and Damon. "He and his grandpa have been working on a drone program that he can operate from his phone. I have the drone," she noted, and she clicked on a few things. "I'm looking to see what distance we've got on this."

"One thousand meters," he stated proudly.

She thought about it. "That's not half bad," she murmured. "What about a line of sight? Does that affect anything?"

"No, it can be from inside. It's all about the strength."

"What about an internet connection?"

"Sure, but it's run off the satellite."

"Of course it is. Everything is these days." Sophia shook her head. "One of these days, the satellites will go down, and the whole world will come to a stop." She faced Wade. "It's too bad this kid's gone down the wrong side of the tracks. He could have done something good."

"What will we do with him now though? That's the question, isn't it? I'd still like to get as much information from them as we can," Wade noted.

"Well, she's already gotten herself full access to everything in my computer," the kid grumbled in disgust. "So I'm not sure that there's anything else I can tell you."

"Maybe not." Wade shrugged. "But we can't just let you go."

"And why not?" he asked.

"Well, for one, you're in the house with a dead guy."

"I didn't know he was the one with cold feet," he protested. "You're not pinning that on me. I didn't have anything to do with his murder."

"But you're involved with the same group who *is* responsible for his murder," she stated. "You just don't get that association, do you?"

He turned silent and pinched his lips together.

She looked over at Damon. "Should we call our agent in the field?"

"Yeah, that's not a bad idea." He stepped away toward a quiet corner.

"What will you do with me?" the kid asked nervously.

"I'm not sure yet." Wade walked over to the other man, who was still unconscious.

"It's this one I want to know more about. What exactly did you guys do to him?" she asked, as she came closer too.

"Hell, I didn't do very much. He said he had some implant that he turned on by tapping his ear, imparting some noise and pressure that was killing my head, and I figured it was something to help knock us out. So, I gave him a good one against the side of the head, and he went down hard."

She stood over the unconscious man and studied him. "Well, I can get everything off him now we know he's Riley Marshall," she noted. "I presume you searched him for anything interesting?"

"I did. Nothing's on him."

"What about vehicles?"

"I haven't gone outside yet," he replied. "I'm still not convinced another drone isn't out there."

"There probably is," she agreed. "Poma more or less said there was. Because, if this guy and his grandpa have been building one, he probably already handed off something to keep the bad guys happy. Which means his boss has likely got a prototype. These guys are marked anyway," she noted. "We should just leave Poma here."

"Yeah, you should," the kid replied, eagerly trying to sit up. "It's not like I'll get into trouble anymore."

"No, you definitely won't, once the police come for your ass," she stated, "and I'm taking your laptop with me." He looked like he wanted to cry. She nodded. "I get that's probably the worst thing I could do to you," she said, with a head shake. "But I still haven't got everything off it that I might want."

"What do you want now?" he asked bitterly. "To take all my inventions too?"

"If I thought they'd do us any good, I would. Spoils of war to the winner and all that." She stepped closer to the unconscious prisoner, tilting her head as she studied him. Seeing something odd, she dropped to his side. "Did you see this?" she asked, and she pointed it out to Wade. "This is the implant. I'm afraid it's doing something to him on the inside."

"Like what?"

She reached down and placed two fingers against his neck, then looked up at Wade in shock.

He swore and dropped down beside her. "Shit." He settled back on his hips.

"What? What is it?" the kid asked. By the looks on their faces, he was terrified now. "You killed him?"

"No, I didn't kill him, though I'm pretty sure that the implant had something to do with it," she murmured. She turned to Wade. "When you hit him, it could have released something that leached into his brain."

"It's probably a fail-safe on their part," he muttered. "What kind of people actually put shit like that in someone's head?"

"I designed it," the kid said proudly.

She looked at him. "Jesus Christ. They put one in your head too, didn't they?"

He nodded. "Of course. It's cutting edge."

"Yeah, cutting edge. You do realize that they killed him, using the implant, right? They probably realized something was going on here and took him out. At least I've got the data from the systems and the frequencies," she noted. "The kid's responsible for that too."

"Which makes him not so innocent at all." Damon sneered in disgust.

"Nope, not at all," she murmured. "At the same time, he's a pretty small fish, and we've got his plans and designs, so if we want to take anything, we can. The biggest problem is, what are we doing with this dead guy here and the body upstairs? Is somebody coming here to clean up the mess?"

Damon moved in closer to Sophia, so the Poma kid wouldn't hear, and whispered to her, "MI6 will come, but

Jonas wants us to leave the crime scene first. He'll talk to us later."

Wade looked at her and asked quietly, under his breath, "Can you track something from that chip in his head?"

She looked over at the kid. "Who's got the master tracks on these chips? Are you keeping the numbers in your head?"

He shrugged. "They're on my laptop," he stated. "Why?"

"Because there's a good chance that the chip in your head will go off next," she replied, "and we'd like to track the chip back to the guys doing this."

He stared at her. "You think the implant in my head will go off?"

"Didn't you design it that way?"

He nodded slowly. "They've got like a trace amount of mercury on the inside. Just a small amount—but enough to poison the brain pretty fast." He shifted farther away from the dead guy beside him on the floor. "Jesus, he's really dead?"

"Yep, dead as a doornail," she said, "just like you'll be soon."

He glared at her. "Stop saying that."

"Why?" she asked reasonably. "You're a small fish to these guys, *Billy the Kid*, and, as long as they already have everything that you've done for them, what do they care if you live or die? It's to their benefit if you die because then they don't have to worry about you saying anything. And thanks for telling me where those codes are." She opened the kid's laptop and started digging. "Got them," she confirmed. "So it's just a matter of sorting out the identities. We've got eight tags so eight people with implants, counting the two here."

She turned and looked at the kid. "So six left. So, which one is this though?" She tapped one of the icons on the screen, and a weird *ping* filled the air. She looked over at him. "Can you feel that?"

He shrugged. "No, of course not. They're not supposed to be anything you can feel. The whole point of them is that they're subtle."

"Yeah, so if I play around with this, it won't cause any pain or anything, right?"

"No," he replied, "it's in my head."

"Yeah, but you didn't care about this guy who died because of what was in his head."

"It's not my fault they decided he was a loser."

She just gave an unhappy sigh. "Talk about stupid." She looked at the eight icons again. "I'll do a test track of one these implants right now from here," she noted. "Pick one, kid. Is one more trackable than another?"

"Anyone local," the kid replied.

"So let me see." She brought up locations. "Two are here in Liverpool, in this house with me. The dead guy and you, the soon-to-be-dead guy. One is in Sheffield, England," she noted. "Two are in Belgium. And, wow, look at this. We've got one in Iran and two in Paris."

"Right." Damon nodded. "Find the one in Sheffield."

At that, she opened it up and turned it on. "Well, it's buzzing," she noted. "We should have a location here within seconds."

The kid protested. "That's not your software," he said. "I built that."

"I'm really proud of you too," she noted absentmindedly. "Too bad you didn't decide to build something with a safeguard for yourself."

He frowned. "I told you that they need me. I'm the only one who can run that shit."

"Yeah, well, I just did," she argued, glancing at him. "So really, how hard can it be?"

He stared at her. "You turned it on, but you didn't do any tweaking or anything to it."

"No, but do they need you to do that? Or did you build it, and now that they've got it, they're good, and they don't need you anymore?"

"Of course they need me," he repeated, yet frowned.

He was getting a little desperate to come up with a reason. "Why do they need you exactly?" she asked again. "Who else has control over these?"

"Well, I had to give my boss control," he replied, and then he paled. "Which also means he likely told his boss."

"Yep." She nodded. "I've got your icon here already, as one of these two Liverpool icons. Obviously they haven't done anything with your implant, but these other six, that'll be interesting to check. First, let's find out who the guy in Sheffield is." She looked over at Poma. "Did you meet anybody else?"

He shook his head. "No, I didn't."

She looked over at Damon. "There's at least one guy in Paris."

"It would be nice if we got him alive, at least long enough to ask questions." Damon looked over at Wade, who shrugged.

"Hey, I didn't kill this one," Wade said. "I knocked him out and maybe that either turned off the device in his head or set off the failsafe portion of the device in his head. Maybe like a panic alarm goes off, and they decided to just jump the gun on it and make sure he didn't survive."

"Of course they did," the kid replied. He was back on the offensive. "You're the idiots."

"Yeah, you keep telling me that," Sophia stated, "but then I keep finding more in your computer. So, do you want to come clean for a change?"

He looked at her. "I did everything you asked. I also did everything they asked. I built what they asked me to build, so there's no reason for you to hurt me. There's no reason for them to hurt me either. This is a simple business transaction."

She sighed, then sat back and looked at him. "I'm not so sure about that, but—" Just then she looked at the locator on her screen. "We've got a location." She brought it up, then started to swear.

"What's the matter?" Wade asked, racing to her side.

"Not only is he in town," she noted, "but he's here in this house."

WADE TOOK ONE look at her face and then bolted for the door, Damon right behind him. She wanted to call after them to double-check the guy who they thought was dead because that could be another scenario. "Why the hell did you name the icons this way?" she asked Poma, not expecting a rational reply.

But, as she checked the computer, she saw that one icon shifting. Thank goodness none of the others were in transit. She pulled out her phone, calling Wade. "It's moving downstairs." The two men raced out to the main floor. "What the hell? Did he just crawl in from somewhere?"

"Obviously the implant icons are labeled as cities instead

of names. Protecting the guilty and all that." She sent a glare to Poma. "Therefore, not their current location necessarily. Which can only be accessed by initiating a tracking sequence. So none of the implants are *live* until I do a trace." She again glared at Poma. "It's not the dead guy with me," she noted. "And I doubt it's the dead guy upstairs because this icon is still moving."

"Good enough." Wade and Damon set up positions, as they watched and listened. They heard an odd sound but coming from another room. Wade frowned, then headed to the kitchen, Damon on his heels. They found a service elevator, something he hadn't seen in operation in a very long time. As he studied it, he realized it was more of a laundry chute, designed to get linens from the main floor to the basement and then on upstairs. He sighed, then pointed it out.

Damon immediately nodded.

They hid themselves on either side of it and waited. Sure enough, the door slid open just a tiny little bit. Then it moved a few more inches, while somebody checked out the lay of the land. With his heart in his throat, Wade waited, until the guy jumped free. Immediately Damon had a hand at the intruder's throat, and he was slammed up against the wall. "Nice of you to drop in."

The guy started swearing heavily.

Damon just smiled. "Hey, this is all good. We're happy to have company." He shared a knowing glance with Wade, recognizing this guy as Jamison Delaware.

"I don't know what you're talking about," he snapped. Just like that, his knee came up hard against Damon's groin, which he immediately blocked, then the visitor punched Damon alongside his head.

"Whoa, whoa, whoa." Wade jumped in and pulled the guy's arms back beside his head. "Stop moving, or I will knock you out cold." Wade was about to punch him out, when he suddenly stopped dead in the tracks, "Oh, shit, I forgot."

"What are you talking about?" Jamison asked, as he struggled in Damon's and now Wade's grasps. "Forgot what?"

"That thing in your buddy Riley's head exploded when I hit him, killing him."

Jamison looked at Wade and frowned. "I don't know what you're talking about. This is my house, so what the hell are you guys doing here?"

"I don't think so, Jamison," Damon replied.

Wade noted the surprise on Jamison's face, at knowing his name. "The owner of this house is William Poma, currently on holiday. Have you spoken to your brother Thomas lately?" Wade asked him.

Jamison froze. "Who the hell are you two?"

"Somebody who wants to talk to you," Damon replied. And they shoved him forward into the other room with the kid.

As soon as he saw the Poma kid, Jamison swore, keeping up his charade. "What the hell is this?" he asked. "Why is everybody in my house?"

"We're not that stupid," Damon replied.

Sophia frowned when she saw the newcomer. "Hi, Jamison."

The guy gave them all a sly look. "Yeah, you are stupid," he spat. "We've got you running circles around your tail."

"And you are Jamison Delaware," she told him, then turned to Wade. "The two forging brothers who are known associates of the Poma kid here."

Wade nodded.

Damon smiled. "We're cutting off your legs. Eventually you'll run out of people."

"Not for a hell of a long time."

Wade shook his head. "I don't know. Have you spoken to your brother lately?" When Jamison refused to answer his question, Wade continued. "People on your side are dropping like flies. Especially the hired hands, the local help."

Jamison jerked his head to Wade. "Do you know why we're after your team?"

"Nope. No idea."

Jamison shook his head. "Idiots."

"Okay," Wade said. "I'll bite. Why?"

"Have you ever heard the phrase 'there can only be one?'"

At that, Wade and Damon looked at him. "Only one what?"

Jamison laughed and laughed. "You're the idiots who don't know anything. You've got nothing on me. I didn't do nothing to anybody." He looked down at the guy on the floor. "Jesus, did you kill Riley?"

"No, it was that thing in your heads," Wade replied.

Jamison looked at him and frowned. "Ain't nothing in my head, so I really wouldn't think anything of it. And, once again, you guys are just making shit up. But then governments do that, don't they?"

"Lots of governments do, yeah," Damon noted. "But what's that got to do with us?"

The guy looked at him and laughed. "You don't even understand what the hell is going on here, do you?"

"Nope, I sure don't," Damon replied.

"Well, you were terminated," he stated, and calmly and with certainty he unraveled the mystery. "But unfortunately you apparently didn't get the message. That's all it is. You know too much."

"And what is your role in that?" Damon asked, an eyebrow raised. "Because obviously you guys suck at your job."

"Well, it's not our job to take you out." Jamison laughed. "We're just watching you and relaying information to the people tracking you. They have some unusual methods that they're trying."

"Not so unusual," Damon noted. "And, so far, they apparently aren't working. We've got seven of you guys down, and our team is still here. With those implants in your heads, you and the Poma kid are next. So that'll be nine of you dead. Oh"—Damon raised his finger—"I forgot. One of the dead is your brother, in the crawl space on the second floor."

Jamison hesitated, schooled his expression. "All of you are in their sights." He grinned. "I don't know what kind of a weird freakish group you guys are, but they wanted to make sure that brain dead meant completely dead."

"Too bad they failed at that." Sophia stood and walked over.

"Who are you anyway?" he asked. "You must be Tasha."

"No, not Tasha."

"Mera?"

"Nope, wrong again," Wade interrupted. "Mera is dead. You guys got some of the admins, but the rest of us? Not so much." Wade studied Jamison's face, seeing the undercurrents evident from hearing of his brother's death. "Apparently you guys don't know what the hell you're up against."

"Well, I don't necessarily know all the details," he admitted, "Even if you take me down, that doesn't stop the rest of us."

"Maybe not." Wade shrugged. "But we'll turn you in and use you as leverage to get a little something for ourselves out of this deal."

The guy sniggered at that. "And, for all you know, I'm transmitting all this to them right now." At that, he turned a sly look toward Sophia. "I'll be sure to tell them about you."

She studied him for a long moment. "Well, I can see that you're being tracked, but transmitting? I'm not so sure about that." She frowned.

"Because you don't know anything." The kid tied up on the ground laughed. "I told you that I'm good."

"Well, you better not be that good," she replied, as she walked back over to his laptop. Sure enough, she found a signal. She immediately killed it and looked over at Damon. "There was a signal, but I don't know if it was tracking, transmitting, or what, but it's dead now. We probably ought to get out of here, just in case."

Damon nodded. "You're right on that. Let's go load them up." He got the kid to his feet, while she grabbed her stuff and the kid's laptop and headed to the front door. She stopped there. "I wish I had a little more confirmation that a drone won't be waiting out there, ready to pick us off," she muttered.

"Hold tight," Damon replied. "If you want to hang on to this guy, I'll go grab the vehicle."

She looked at Poma, shook her head. "How about I grab the vehicle and pull up closer to the front? You guys hang on to them, and I'll be right back." Ignoring her misgivings, she raced out to the truck and hopped in, feeling a sense of relief as soon as she was inside the truck, and she pulled up to the front of the house without incident.

Wade watched as she pulled the truck near. Motioning Damon to go first, they stepped out. But the kid only made one step away from the front door, then made a weird gasp. Reaching his hand to his head, he collapsed to his knees.

"Shit," Damon muttered. "The kid didn't even make it as far as the truck."

"What the hell?" Jamison yelled.

"It's that implant in his head," she called from the truck.

The kid then fell forward onto his face. Damon checked for a pulse, then shook his head. He dragged the body back inside, then turned and looked at Jamison, standing beside Wade and looking decidedly pale. "You still want to be the tough guy?"

"Absolutely. That's my team out there. They won't take me out because I'm on their side."

"Well, we'll see, won't we?" Damon stated in disgust. Then he shifted, pushing Jamison out ahead. As they headed outside, it took only about ten steps before Jamison dropped to his knees, then pitched face forward too.

Just then, a drone fired at them from above.

Wade and Damon dashed inside the truck, taking the front seat. Sophia had shifted to the back seat, with the kid's laptop opened, and Wade called to her. "Can you shut down that drone?" he asked urgently.

"I'm trying to, damn it."

He watched as her fingers flew across the keyboard, then finally she said, "Got it!" She punched a button, and immediately the drone crashed to the ground.

"Can you tell if we're being tracked?"

"Not by that drone anyway. I crashed it."

"So we can't get anything off it, can we?"

"No." She shook her head. "Probably not. But no telling what else we'll find on the laptop. We'll definitely get more information as I dig. A ton is on here."

"Good enough. Home it is then. Let's go."

As they raced away toward home, she looked over at Wade. "This really is a life-and-death scenario for you, isn't it?"

"It appears to be," Wade replied. "I told you. You don't have to be here just to hook up with me."

"Too late," she said.

He looked at her in the rearview mirror and frowned.

Damon sat in the passenger seat. "Hey, don't worry about me being here." He grinned, clearly trying to go with humor.

"I wasn't," Wade replied, with a laugh.

She smiled but thought about everything that he would try to convince her of. She didn't know how to tell him that she was in for the long haul. It would take time, which was something that they may or may not have. But she wanted whatever days they could have to be together, even if they were cut short.

As they got back to the base, Damon walked inside and took Tasha in his arms.

Whereas Wade dragged Sophia down to their room. "You need to go home," he told her. "Pack up your stuff and go, so at least you'll live to see another day."

"And you?" she asked calmly. She finally realized that Wade really was all about looking after her and making sure that she stayed safe. "You realize, of course, that there's no guarantee even now that I would be safe."

He swallowed. "But we can hope that you are. If you stay here, you're not."

"Well, so far, we did lose Wilson and Mera. However, more of the bad guys are dying," she noted. "Remember that."

Wade frowned, and she nodded. He felt his own energy draining as the shock and the adrenaline of the encounter wore off. "Jesus, I'm about done." Wade reached out a shaky hand.

"Exactly," she agreed, "so you need me."

"And what exactly can you do for me?" he asked.

"Well, I don't know, but maybe you should start using some more of the energy I've been giving you." He looked at her in shock and surprise. She nodded. "I might not know how all this works, but I haven't been an innocent for a very long time. So, when you needed energy, I made it available."

"What do you mean, you made it available?"

"I called out to you mentally and told you to use it. I don't know if you heard me or not, but you definitely started using it. But I have an almost unlimited source because, well, I don't have to burn it as quickly as you do."

He thought about it for a moment. "Wait. So you were the source of that huge warm rush of energy that came to me?"

She nodded. "I presume so. Why don't you test it and see?" In a teasing voice, she asked, "You're the one who can see signatures, right?"

He smiled, then closed his eyes and searched. Looking for her energy, he recognized it right off the bat. He opened his eyes almost immediately. "I don't know why I didn't realize it was you before."

"Because it was part of your own energy really," she noted. "Love is like that." He widened his eyes at her wording, and she just nodded. "There's only one reason I would be here right now," she explained, "but I'm not so sure I want to be here if it's a one-way street. Therefore, you need to be straight with me."

He wrapped her up in his arms, held her close. "It's definitely not a one-way street," he whispered. "I just wanted you safe. Once I realized that everything was turning into such a big mess, I knew I couldn't take the chance and put you at risk like that."

"We had something very special," she admitted. "Something I've never experienced with anybody else."

"I know … I know," he whispered. "I felt the same way, but I couldn't imagine having something so special only to get you killed because of it."

"I get it." She reached up and kissed his cheek. "But you don't get to make that decision all on your own," she murmured. "There are two of us in this now. Not just you alone."

"And if something happens to you?" he asked, his voice shaking.

She reached up, wrapped her arms around his neck. "What if something happens to you?" He frowned. She nodded. "Exactly. It's the same thing. But neither of us wants the other to get hurt, so let's do our best to be safe together."

"Fine," he said, giving in. "You can stay, but damn it. If something happens to you, I—"

She reached up and put one finger on his lips, and, searching his face, saw the exact same emotions that she felt in her heart. "For the same reason that you could use my energy," she replied, "there's no reason that we can't be strong enough together to beat this. I don't know what life will bring for us," she murmured, "but I'm willing to give it our all to make sure we find out."

He wrapped his arms around her and kissed her deeply. "Got it," he said. "Fine. No more talk about you leaving."

"Good." She nodded. "How about no more talk about when you walked away too?" she added. "I will let that go."

"You will?" he murmured. "Thank you. I'm so sorry I hurt you."

"Me too," she murmured. "It sucked."

He laughed. "But at least now we know where we stand." With a cheeky smile, he pulled his T-shirt up over his head.

"You're the one who just told me that you were tired and worn out." She smiled back at him. "I'm pretty damn sure that means you need to have a little bit of time to yourself to unwind."

"So what does that mean exactly? You'll go out there and work, while I'm in here?" He waggled his eyebrows.

"Hell no. I'm here with you. And we both need a bit of time together," she stated. "Just like we all do. And I have no idea where Terk is."

"Probably recharging," he replied, with a big smile.

"Man, have you got a lot to explain," she stated. "I've picked up some things, but still, I don't know so much."

"I understand." Wade nodded. "And it's tough to take it all in, even parsed out, but we'll get there." Then he lowered his head and kissed her. But that wasn't enough for her, so she wrapped her arms around him and walked backward until her legs hit the edge of the bed, and she just fell back, pulling him with her. He came down hard on top of her with an *oomph*.

She absorbed the impact, then slipped her tongue into his mouth, her own appetite suddenly racing, as she realized what was once again within her grasp. She whispered, "Love me."

"Always," he whispered and lowered his head.

This time, his passionate kiss took them to depths that she'd only ever experienced once before—with him. By the time she surfaced for air, she'd already been completely stripped of her clothing and was even now being repositioned, so he had better access. She chuckled, opening her thighs wide, her arms wrapped around him, literally holding on for dear life.

He slowly and delicately slipped down and entered her. But she grabbed him hard, and, holding his hips, she plunged up, while pulling him down, seating him deep within her. He shuddered in her arms, softly dropped his forehead against hers, and whispered, "We could have done this more slowly."

"Next time," she murmured. "Next time. Right now this is all about us. And there has been a long enough wait as it is." And, with that, she flipped him on his back. "You're the injured one."

And she started to ride.

He didn't argue; he didn't do anything except arch his back and his hips, while his hands stroked up and down across her breasts. "If this is what it means to be injured," he replied, "I won't argue quite so much next time."

She chuckled and leaned forward, then placed her hands on his chest and picked up the pace into a hard and fast ride. When the tremors started deep within, she cried out.

Then he reached up, grabbed her hips, and plunged up hard several times, sending her trembling over the edge, following in a fury of groans himself.

She collapsed on top of him. "I don't know if that

charges energy," she said, "or if it drains it. But I sure hope it's charging it."

He chuckled. "I think, in this case, it's probably doing a whole lot of both."

"Well, I don't think that's bad then," she murmured, "because it's never been like that with anybody else."

"Good," he murmured. "It should always be special between two people who care."

"Oh, I care," she replied, "but apparently that care translated into a need to be looked after."

"Nope," he stated, "but you didn't recognize the same emotions in me, plus the need to keep you safe."

"But not anymore," she added. "Right?" He grinned, then rolled over and gave her a long hard kiss. As she relaxed into the bed, they heard a commotion outside. She froze while Wade bolted to his feet, quickly throwing on his clothes.

"We will get some time together, right?"

"We will," he replied, "but obviously not right now." Fully dressed, he pulled open the door, even as she was scrambling to get her T-shirt down.

Wade stepped out into the hallway and right there in front of him, leaning on a crutch and the wall, was Gage. Wade wrapped his arms around his old friend. "Jesus. Are you sure you're supposed to be here?"

"I don't know," Gage said, "but the damn signals I got were crazy." He shook his head. "I don't know what it was. I kept trying to shut them down, but they were zigzagging all over the place. Like drones and receivers and I don't know what all." He shook his head. "I snipped as many as I could. Distancing myself from the chaos."

Behind him, Sophia asked, "*Snipped?*"

He looked over at her and frowned.

She smiled. "I'm Sophia."

Gage looked at Wade, shrugged. "Yeah, snipped. I wasn't sure what I was doing, but I saw all these transmissions, and I just kept shutting them down. Seemed like they were transmissions to people's heads, if that makes any sense." He frowned at her. "I have no idea where or what they were, but they didn't feel natural, and they didn't feel right," he stated, "so I shut them off. Not sure what good that did, if anything, but it was self-preservation on my part."

"Well, good timing if you did," she noted. "Maybe we weren't looking for the same boogeyman we thought we were." When Gage and Wade turned and looked at her for more explanation, she shrugged. "It's quite possible... I mean, if I knew what the hell was fully going on with you guys, it might be quite possible," she replied, with a laugh, "that maybe we had a little bit of unexpected help with the implants that we didn't realize we needed."

Damon joined them. "We thought the help was actually the enemy's actions." Damon helped Gage over to a chair to sit down. "Glad to have you here, buddy."

Just then Terk bolted to his feet from his charging position on the floor, just as Gage sat down. "You know you could have stayed where you were," Terk snapped at Gage in exasperation. "That took a ton out of me to help you get here."

"Yeah, sorry about that, boss, but you know I'm a little bit of a bull in a china shop, once I get an idea in my head."

"Yeah. Isn't that the truth."

Wade gave Gage another bro hug. "Regardless, it's damn good to see you alive, well, and here. Not a moment too soon either."

CHAPTER 13

SOPHIA LOOKED FROM Terk to Gage. "Jesus, you've been funneling energy enough to keep him on his feet?"

"Yeah, and, now that he's here, he'll have a hell of a lot of healing to do," Terk noted. "And we won't count on his abilities, while he's doing it. Because, if I'm helping him, I can't help anybody else. Which is why"—Terk turned and glared at his friend—"I was trying to get Gage to stay where he was."

"Yeah, but I couldn't because it was evident that you guys were under attack. I could sense that and could feel it at the same time," he replied. "And you know me. I can't let you guys get hurt."

"I get that," Wade admitted. "But, wow, it would have been nice to have known that was you canceling these software implants."

"Well, it was one of the few things I could do," he stated. "I'm still not sure what they were connected to."

"They were connected to people," Sophia noted. "When you interrupted the signal, it released a trace amount of mercury in their brains, and it killed them."

Gage looked at her in surprise. "Please tell me that they were bad guys at least."

"That I can do." She nodded. "The worst, definitely."

He smiled. "Well, I guess it doesn't really matter then."

He looked over at Tasha. "Tasha, honey, save me. I don't suppose there happens to be a bed around here that I could crash on, is there?"

She hopped up and walked over and gave him a big long hug. "There is, but let me see if there is a clear passage to get you there." When she returned, she looked at the others. "Okay, the path is clear, but it'll likely take all of us to get him there." Then she led the way, as the men half carried and half dragged Gage, a big square block of a man, into the nearest unoccupied bedroom.

When they all returned, Sophia said, "I don't even think I have the ability to formulate all the questions I have to ask right now." She shrugged. "For the record, I just want to say that I'm really glad you guys are on our side."

At that, Terk laughed. "Welcome to the team."

Wade was so happy, and his words made everything else seem inconsequential. "Welcome to my life!"

EPILOGUE

GAGE OPENED HIS eyes. He was pretty damn sure that Terk had done something to knock him out. He was just afraid that he may have been knocked out for a few weeks. He slowly sat up, shifted his gaze, and realized that he felt damn good. He got up, went to the bathroom, and, when he walked out to the main room, there was a sudden silence, as everybody turned to look at him. Then Tasha hopped to her feet from where she'd been sitting with Damon and came running. He opened his arms and held her gently. "Am I correct to assume that old doofus finally broke down and did the right thing?"

She chuckled. "Well, it might have taken a little bit of convincing," she teased.

Damon rolled his eyes at that. "Hardly." He got up, walked over to Gage, and asked, "How are you feeling?"

"Like I've been hit by a cement truck, then dumped into a river and shaken off a little bit," he replied. "How do I look?"

"About like that." Damon grinned.

Gage walked forward, then shifted, rolling his shoulders front and back. "Actually I don't feel all that bad. Just kind of stiff. How long have I been out?"

"A couple days," said another woman, sitting off to the side. He looked at her, his brain trying to find the info.

"Sophia, was it?"

"Yes, I am Sophia." She walked over and shook his hand. "I'm with Wade."

Gage looked at Wade in surprise.

Wade shrugged. "You remember the night that we were attacked about a year ago? I was out with her that night," he explained. "I was supposed to go back the next night for dinner, and, of course, I didn't show up."

"Of course not," Gage stated, in complete understanding. "We don't like to bring danger to other people. Especially those we care about."

"Well in this case," she replied, "I've been working with Levi's team for the last year on a few jobs here and there. The minute I found this guy again, I didn't let go."

"That bad, huh?"

"Well, that good." She smiled a cheeky grin. "I get why he walked, but he doesn't get that opportunity again."

At that, Gage burst out laughing. "Okay, that sounds great," he replied, happy to be conscious and to be feeling better. "Now that I'm alive, do you have any news? An update at least?"

"A lot of dead bad guys. They are killing them off for us. So not a whole lot of usable intel yet," Terk replied from the side. He shifted, stood, stretched, and walked closer, studying his friend.

"Thanks," Gage said sincerely to Terk. "I don't think I would have survived that."

"No, I don't think you would have either. It's been touch-and-go for all of us," Terk murmured.

"So no intel?"

Just then a message beeped on Terk's phone. He pulled it out and read it. "Anybody know a Lorelei?"

"We all do. Lorelei worked in the government," Gage stated.

At that, Terk froze, turned, and looked at him. "Your Lorelei?"

"Well, she's hardly mine," he replied, "but she's my contact, yes. We all know her but didn't see her much, as she's stateside."

"Well, I think that same Lorelei has a message for us. He pulled it up and read from it. *"You are in danger, all of you. Go under and stay safe."*

"Isn't that a little late for a warning?"

"Or it's a new warning," Sophia suggested.

"And that's possible too." Gage frowned, as his finger hovered over the message. "Let me send her a message."

"Wait. Does she even know you're alive?" Terk asked Gage.

"No, I don't know that she does." Gage shook his head. "And I guess we don't want her to know."

"Most people know I'm alive, and that's partly why we're still being hunted," Terk explained.

"Of course they do," Gage agreed. "You always were the hardest one to kill."

"Damn right," Terk murmured. He sent Lorelei a message. **Can you help?**

When his phone rang, he was given a series of numbers to dial on his end. Eyebrows raised, he quickly dialed them.

When he was connected, a woman answered. "This is a secure line."

"Lorelei?"

"Yes," she answered, her voice heavy. "Oh my God, Terk, I'm so sorry."

"Do you have any idea what happened?" he asked.

"I don't know all the details, no," she replied, "but I overhead something about your team being wiped out."

"Well, depends what *wiped out* means," Terk stated.

"I only just heard, and that's why I'm calling you."

"Yeah, why's that?" he asked, putting it on Speakerphone.

"Have you"—she stopped—"Have you heard from Gage?"

"Ah," Terk said, looking over at Gage. "Why?"

"Because I really don't want to think that he's dead," she replied. "But now that I heard that something happened to your team, I'm really worried about him."

"And with good reason," Terk said. "Do you know what happened to the team?"

"No, I don't. They were just talking about a major attack. And I don't understand why," she explained. "You were supposed to be disbanded. I was hoping to hear from Gage once he was done there. 'Cause I know he's always been against any type of relationship while he worked for that division."

"That's because of the danger involved." Although Terk had come to believe—for himself, as well as for the members of his team—that finding the right partner, the one who could meld in with the rest of them, was a plus, not a minus. Actually a good grounding mechanism for these guys, who carried extra-big loads of stress and expectations and levels of success on their shoulders. And having exceptional women on board, who could be mates and part of the team too, could bring along their own special skills? *Wow.* Terk shook his head that he and the guys had not seen this particular element of their lives in a more open manner.

"I get that. I really do," she replied anxiously. "Please tell me. Have you heard from him?"

"And what difference would it make now?" Terk asked, frowning.

"I'm in Manchester," she said abruptly.

At that, Terk's warning signals went up. "You're in Manchester?"

Gage instinctively took a step forward.

"Yes," she confirmed. "I came over, hoping to talk to Gage, as soon as you guys had completed your last day on the job. I flew in that Friday. And then I found out about the team."

Silence shocked Gage and Terkel, as they stared at each other.

"And I know you won't believe this," she added, "but I was hit by a car that next morning. I've just been released from the hospital myself."

Everybody froze.

"Seriously?"

"Yeah," she confirmed in a small voice. "I don't know if it's connected."

"I would say it's a little too closely timed not to be connected," Terk replied. "I need to meet you. Where do you suggest?"

"I don't know." She hesitated. "I've got a safe line 'cause I'm the one who used to arrange them at work," she noted. "However, I don't know about a safe place. I've checked into a hotel, so maybe here."

"That works." Terk studied Gage, who was motionless in front of him. Terk quickly wrote down her address. "We're on our way." Then he hung up. He looked over at Gage. "What do you think?"

"Let's go." He walked to the door. "That son of a bitch.

It's not just us who were attacked, it sounds like everybody who had anything to do with us too."

"Yeah, and we've lost our government access and team support as well," Terk noted. "This is bigger than just us. But it still doesn't change the fact that we're the only ones, *really* the only ones who are in any position to fix this."

Gage nodded. "Damn good thing I'm feeling better, huh?"

"Yeah, damn good thing," Terkel agreed, with a wry eye roll. "Now you need to stay healthy, please? The more of you guys who go down, the less I have for myself."

"That's not true," Gage argued, whacking him on the shoulder. "It's just you're too stuffy and don't want to take it from anybody else."

Terkel laughed. "Whatever," he replied. "Let's go. Do you think she'll be happy to see you?"

"Damn, I hope so," he stated. "It was good to hear her voice."

"And what about the worry in her voice?"

"Well, she's right. I was hoping to see her afterward," he noted. "We hadn't discussed anything formally. She did have holidays coming up so ... I would have waited a day or two."

Terkel nodded. "Apparently you guys all had plans."

"What were your plans?" Gage asked his friend.

"I would go to Texas to visit my brother. Now, if and whenever I get safely from here," he added, "there's a woman I need to meet."

"A woman?" Gage asked, turning and looking at him. Terk explained, and Gage's jaw dropped. "Seriously? A stranger carrying your child? You know she could be behind all of this."

"No. She's suffered at the hands of these assholes herself. She's also still in a coma, or at least was the last two days that

I talked to Ice."

"Jesus, man, that sucks." Gage couldn't believe the lengths these people had gone to. "Especially when I know children are an issue for you."

"I know, but, until we get a little more information, I'm not bringing her into any more danger by going there myself."

"And why her? What did she do to attract their attention?"

Terk shrugged. "At the moment we have no idea. And, of course, we've been a little too busy to find out more on her."

"But you know something," Gage prodded.

Terk nodded, grabbed his jacket, and looked at the rest of the team.

Tasha nodded at Sophia. "We will do a deeper dive into that."

"Yeah, you go meet Lorelei," Sophia said. "You guys solve that problem, and we'll get to work here."

"Done," Terkel noted, and together the two men left.

As Gage walked out the rear door, casting one last glance back at the small group, he had to wonder if it was just the four of them left. What the hell had happened, and how would they get to the bottom of this? Then he looked at Terkel striding forward, and Gage realized the *hows* didn't matter. Because Gage could count on one guarantee. And that was that Terkel was determined to solve this. And he'd solve it in such a way that everybody else would pay the price for having crossed them.

And Gage was good with that.

This concludes Book 2 of Terkel's Team: Wade's War.

Read about Gage's Goal: Terkel's Team, Book 3

Terkel's Team: Gage's Goal
(Book #3)

Welcome to a brand-new series from *USA Today* best-selling author Dale Mayer, where dark-ops SEALs have special senses and skills, needed to solve intrigue, betrayal, and ... murder. A series with all the elements you've come to love, plus so much more, ... including psychics!

Gage hadn't told the rest of his team, but he'd planned to meet up with Lorelei after their team disbanded. A little one-on-one time was needed to see if all the sparks they'd felt over the last few years were the real thing. He'd deliberately avoided getting involved with anyone he worked with, so this seemed like the perfect opportunity. Until all the team is decimated ...

Lorelei was in Manchester, hoping to run into Gage, but after a car accident that sent her to hospital with an injured leg, she had no idea what had happened to the others, until Terk contacted her. Once he realized what had befallen her, he figured out that her accident was likely no accident and probably the same potential annihilation that his team had experienced. Terk coaxes Lorelei to live in their temporary new headquarters, where she finds out Gage hadn't contacted her by choice but because he couldn't.

Now on the mend, Gage is determined to keep her safe, only that's much easier said than done, as the attacks turn on her and just ... won't ... stop.

Find Book 3 here!
To find out more visit Dale Mayer's website.
http://smarturl.it/DMTTGageUniversal

Magnus: Shadow Recon (Book #1)

Deep in the permafrost of the Arctic, a joint task force, comprised of over one dozen countries, comes together to level up their winter skills. A mix of personalities, nationalities, and egos bring out the best—and the worst—as these globally elite men and women work and play together. They rub elbows with hardy locals and a group of scientists gathered close by ...

One fatality is almost expected with this training. A second is tough but not a surprise. However, when a third goes missing? It's hard to not be suspicious. When the missing man is connected to one of the elite Maverick team members and is a special friend of Lieutenant Commander Mason Callister? All hell breaks loose …

L IEUTENANT COMMANDER MASON Callister walked into the private office and stood in front of retired Navy Commander Doran Magellan.

"Mason, good to see you."

Yet the dry tone of voice, and the scowl pinching the silver-haired man, all belied his words. Mason had known Doran for over a decade, and their friendship had only grown over time.

Mason waited, as he watched the other man try to work the new tech phone system on his desk. With his hand circling the air above the black box, he appeared to hit buttons randomly.

Mason held back his amusement but to no avail.

"Why can't a phone be a phone anymore?" the commander snapped, as his glare shifted from Mason to the box and back.

Asking the commander if he needed help wouldn't make the older man feel any better, but sitting here and watching as he indiscriminately punched buttons was a struggle. "Is Helen away?" Mason asked.

"Yes, damn it. She's at lunch, and I need her to be at lunch." The commander's piercing gaze pinned Mason in place. "No one is to know you're here."

Solemn, Mason nodded. "Understood."

"Doran? Is that you?" A crotchety voice slammed into the room through the phone's speakers. "Get away from that damn phone. You keep clicking buttons in my ear. Get

Helen in there to do this."

"No, she can't be here for this."

Silence came first, then a huge groan. "Damn it. Then you should have connected me last, so I don't have to sit here and listen to you fumbling around."

"Go pour yourself a damn drink then," Doran barked. "I'm working on the others."

A snort was his only response.

Mason bit the inside of his lip, as he really tried to hold back his grin. The retired commander had been hell on wheels while on active duty, and, even now, the retired part of his life seemed to be more of a euphemism than anything.

"Damn things ..."

Mason looked around the dark mahogany office and the walls filled with photos, awards, medals. A life of purpose, accomplishment. And all of that had only piqued his interest during the initial call he'd received, telling him to be here at this time.

"Ah, got it."

Mason's eyebrows barely twitched, as the commander gave him a feral grin. "I'd rather lead a warship into battle than deal with some of today's technology."

As he was one of only a few commanders who'd been in a position to do such a thing, it said much about his capabilities.

And much about current technology.

The commander leaned back in his massive chair and motioned to the cart beside Mason. "Pour three cups."

Interesting. Mason walked a couple steps across the rich tapestry-style carpet and lifted the silver service to pour coffee into three very down-to-earth-looking mugs.

"Black for me."

Mason picked up two cups and walked one over to Doran.

"Thanks." He leaned forward and snapped into the phone, "Everyone here?"

Multiple voices responded.

Curiouser and curiouser. Mason recognized several of the voices. Other relics of an era gone by. Although not a one would like to hear that, and, in good faith, it wasn't fair. Mason had thought each of these men were retired, had relinquished power. Yet, as he studied Doran in front of him, Mason had to wonder if any of them actually had passed the baton or if they'd only slid into the shadows. Was this planned with the government's authority? Or were these retirees a shadow group to the government?

The tangible sense of power and control oozed from Doran's words, tone, stature—his very pores. This man might be heading into his sunset years—based on a simple calculation of chronological years spent on the planet—but he was a long way from being out of the action.

"Mason ..." Doran began.

"Sir?"

"We've got a problem."

Mason narrowed his gaze and waited.

Doran's glare was hard, steely hard, with an icy glint. "Do you know the Mavericks?"

Mason's eyebrows shot up. The black ops division was one of those well-kept secrets, so, therefore, everyone knew about it. He gave a decisive nod. "I do."

"And you're involved in the logistics behind the ICE training program in the Arctic, are you not?"

"I am." Now where was the commander going with this?

"Do you know another SEAL by the name of Mountain

Rode? He's been working for the black ops Mavericks." At his own words, the commander shook his head. "What the hell was his mother thinking when she gave him that moniker?"

"She wasn't thinking anything," said the man with a hard voice from behind Mason.

He stiffened slightly, then relaxed as he recognized that voice too.

"She died giving birth to me. And my full legal name is Mountain Bear Rode. It was my father's doing."

The commander glared at the new arrival. "Did I say you could come in?"

"Yes." Mountain's voice was firm, yet a definitive note of affection filled his tone.

That emotion told Mason so much.

The commander harrumphed, then cleared his throat. "Mason, we're picking up a significant amount of chatter over that ICE training. Most of it good. Some of it the usual caterwauling we've come to expect every time we participate in a joint training mission. This one is set to run for six months, then to reassess."

Mason already knew this. But he waited for the commander to get around to why Mason was here, and, more important, what any of this had to do with the mountain of a man who now towered beside him.

The commander shifted his gaze to Mountain, but he remained silent.

Mason noted Mountain was not only physically big but damn imposing and severely pissed, seemingly barely holding back the forces within. His body language seemed to yell, *And the world will fix this, or I'll find the reason why.*

For a moment Mason felt sorry for the world.

Finally a voice spoke through the phone. "Mason, this is Alpha here. I run the Mavericks. We've got a problem with that ICE training center. Mountain, tell him."

Mason shifted to include Mountain in his field of vision. Mason wished the other men on the conference call were in the room too. It was one thing to deal with men you knew and could take the measure of; it was another when they were silent shadows in the background.

"My brother is one of the men who reported for the Artic training three weeks ago."

"Tergan Rode?" Mason confirmed. "I'm the one who arranged for him to go up there. He's a great kid."

A glimmer of a smile cracked Mountain's stony features. He nodded. "Indeed. A bright light in my often dark world. He's a dozen years younger than me, just passed his BUD/s training this spring, and raring to go. Until his raring to go then got up and went."

Oh, shit. Mason's gaze zinged to the commander, who had kicked up his feet to rest atop the big desk. Stocking feet. With Mickey Mouse images dancing on them. Sidetracked, Mason struggled to pull his attention back to Mountain. "Meaning?"

"He's disappeared." Mountain let out a harsh breath, as if just saying that out loud, and maybe to the right people, could allow him to relax—at least a little.

The commander spoke up. "We need your help, Mason. You're uniquely qualified for this problem."

It didn't sound like he was qualified in any way for anything he'd heard so far. "Clarify." His spoken word was simplicity itself, but the tone behind it said he wanted the cards on the table ... now.

Mountain spoke up. "He's the third incident."

Mason's gaze narrowed, as the reports from the training

camp rolled through his mind. "One was Russian. One was from the German SEAL team. Both were deemed accidental deaths."

"No, they weren't."

There it was. The root of the problem in black-and-white. He studied Mountain, aiming for neutrality. "Do you have evidence?"

"My brother did."

"Ah, hell."

Mountain gave a clipped nod. "I'm going to find him."

"Of that I have no doubt," Mason said quietly. "Do you have a copy of the evidence he collected?"

"I have some of it." Mountain held out a USB key. "This is your copy. Top secret."

"We don't have to remind you, Mason, that lives are at stake," Doran added. "Nor do we need another international incident. Consider also that a group of scientists, studying global warming, is close by, and not too far away is a village home to a few hardy locals."

Mason accepted the key, turned to the commander, and asked, "Do we know if this is internal or enemy warfare?"

"We don't know at this point," Alpha replied through the phone. "Mountain will lead Shadow Recon. His mission is twofold. One, find out what's behind these so-called accidents and put a stop to it by any means necessary. Two, locate his brother, hopefully alive."

"And where do I come in?" Mason asked.

"We want you to pull together a special team. The members of Shadow Recon will report to both you and Mountain, just in case."

That was clear enough.

"You'll stay stateside but in constant communication with Mountain—with the caveat that, if necessary, you're on the next flight out."

"What about bringing in other members from the Mavericks?" Mason suggested.

Alpha took this question too, his response coming through via Speakerphone. "We don't have the numbers. The budget for our division has been cut. So we called the commander to pull some strings."

That was Doran's cue to explain further. "Mountain has fought hard to get me on board with this plan, and I'm here now. The navy has a special budget for Shadow Recon and will take care of Mountain and you, Mason, and the team you provide."

"Skills needed?"

"Everything," Mountain said, his voice harsh. "But the biggest is these men need to operate in the shadows, mostly alone, without a team beside them. Too many new arrivals will alert the enemy. If we make any changes to the training program, it will raise alarms. We'll move the men in one or two at a time on the same rotation that the trainees are running right now."

"And when we get to the bottom of this?" Mason looked from the commander back to Mountain.

"Then the training can resume as usual," Doran stated.

Mason immediately churned through the names already popping up in his mind. How much could he tell his men? Obviously not much. Hell, he didn't know much himself. How much time did he have? "Timeline?"

The commander's final word told him of the urgency. "Yesterday."

Find Magnus here!

To find out more visit Dale Mayer's website.

smarturl.it/DMSSRMagnus

Author's Note

Thank you for reading Wade's War: Terkel's Team, Book 2!
If you enjoyed the book, please take a moment and leave a
short review.

Dear reader,

I love to hear from readers, and you can contact me at my
website: www.dalemayer.com or at my Facebook author
page. To be informed of new releases and special offers, sign
up for my newsletter or follow me on BookBub. And if you
are interested in joining Dale Mayer's Reader Group, here is
the Facebook sign up page.
https://smarturl.it/DaleMayerFBGroup

Cheers,
Dale Mayer

Get THREE Free Books Now!

Have you met the SEALS of Honor?

SEALs of Honor Books 1, 2, and 3. Follow the stories of brave, badass warriors who serve their country with honor and love their women to the limits of life and death.

Read Mason, Hawk, and Dane right now for FREE.

Go here and tell me where to send them!
http://smarturl.it/EthanBofB

About the Author

Dale Mayer is a *USA Today* best-selling author, best known for her SEALs military romances, her Psychic Visions series, and her Lovely Lethal Garden cozy series. Her contemporary romances are raw and full of passion and emotion (Broken But … Mending series). Her thrillers will keep you guessing (By Death series), and her romantic comedies will keep you giggling (*It's a Dog's Life*, a stand-alone novella; and the Broken Protocols series, starring Charming Marvin, the cat).

Dale honors the stories that come to her—and some of them are crazy and break all the rules and cross multiple genres!

To go with her fiction, she also writes nonfiction in many different fields, with books available on résumé writing, companion gardening, and the US mortgage system. She has recently published her Career Essentials series. All her books are available in print and ebook format.

Connect with Dale Mayer Online

Dale's Website – www.dalemayer.com
Twitter – @DaleMayer
Facebook – facebook.com/DaleMayer.author
BookBub – bookbub.com/authors/dale-mayer

Also by Dale Mayer

Published Adult Books:

Bullard's Battle
Ryland's Reach, Book 1
Cain's Cross, Book 2
Eton's Escape, Book 3
Garret's Gambit, Book 4
Kano's Keep, Book 5
Fallon's Flaw, Book 6
Quinn's Quest, Book 7
Bullard's Beauty, Book 8
Bullard's Best, Book 9

Terkel's Team
Damon's Deal, Book 1
Wade's War, Book 2
Gage's Goal, Book 3
Calum's Contact, Book 4

Kate Morgan
Simon Says… Hide, Book 1
Simon Says… Jump, Book 2
Simon Says… Ride, Book 3
Simon Says… Scream, Book 4

Hathaway House

Aaron, Book 1

Brock, Book 2

Cole, Book 3

Denton, Book 4

Elliot, Book 5

Finn, Book 6

Gregory, Book 7

Heath, Book 8

Iain, Book 9

Jaden, Book 10

Keith, Book 11

Lance, Book 12

Melissa, Book 13

Nash, Book 14

Owen, Book 15

Percy, Book 16

Hathaway House, Books 1–3

Hathaway House, Books 4–6

Hathaway House, Books 7–9

The K9 Files

Ethan, Book 1

Pierce, Book 2

Zane, Book 3

Blaze, Book 4

Lucas, Book 5

Parker, Book 6

Carter, Book 7

Weston, Book 8

Greyson, Book 9

Rowan, Book 10

Caleb, Book 11

Kurt, Book 12

Tucker, Book 13

Harley, Book 14

Kyron, Book 15

Jenner, Book 16

The K9 Files, Books 1–2

The K9 Files, Books 3–4

The K9 Files, Books 5–6

The K9 Files, Books 7–8

The K9 Files, Books 9–10

The K9 Files, Books 11–12

Lovely Lethal Gardens

Arsenic in the Azaleas, Book 1

Bones in the Begonias, Book 2

Corpse in the Carnations, Book 3

Daggers in the Dahlias, Book 4

Evidence in the Echinacea, Book 5

Footprints in the Ferns, Book 6

Gun in the Gardenias, Book 7

Handcuffs in the Heather, Book 8

Ice Pick in the Ivy, Book 9

Jewels in the Juniper, Book 10

Killer in the Kiwis, Book 11

Lifeless in the Lilies, Book 12

Murder in the Marigolds, Book 13

Nabbed in the Nasturtiums, Book 14

Offed in the Orchids, Book 15

Poison in the Pansies, Book 16

Quarry in the Quince, Book 17

Lovely Lethal Gardens, Books 1–2

Lovely Lethal Gardens, Books 3–4
Lovely Lethal Gardens, Books 5–6
Lovely Lethal Gardens, Books 7–8
Lovely Lethal Gardens, Books 9–10

Psychic Vision Series

Tuesday's Child
Hide 'n Go Seek
Maddy's Floor
Garden of Sorrow
Knock Knock...
Rare Find
Eyes to the Soul
Now You See Her
Shattered
Into the Abyss
Seeds of Malice
Eye of the Falcon
Itsy-Bitsy Spider
Unmasked
Deep Beneath
From the Ashes
Stroke of Death
Ice Maiden
Snap, Crackle...
What If...
Talking Bones
Psychic Visions Books 1–3
Psychic Visions Books 4–6
Psychic Visions Books 7–9

By Death Series
Touched by Death
Haunted by Death
Chilled by Death
By Death Books 1–3

Broken Protocols – Romantic Comedy Series
Cat's Meow
Cat's Pajamas
Cat's Cradle
Cat's Claus
Broken Protocols 1-4

Broken and... Mending
Skin
Scars
Scales (of Justice)
Broken but... Mending 1-3

Glory
Genesis
Tori
Celeste
Glory Trilogy

Biker Blues
Morgan: Biker Blues, Volume 1
Cash: Biker Blues, Volume 2

SEALs of Honor
Mason: SEALs of Honor, Book 1
Hawk: SEALs of Honor, Book 2

Dane: SEALs of Honor, Book 3
Swede: SEALs of Honor, Book 4
Shadow: SEALs of Honor, Book 5
Cooper: SEALs of Honor, Book 6
Markus: SEALs of Honor, Book 7
Evan: SEALs of Honor, Book 8
Mason's Wish: SEALs of Honor, Book 9
Chase: SEALs of Honor, Book 10
Brett: SEALs of Honor, Book 11
Devlin: SEALs of Honor, Book 12
Easton: SEALs of Honor, Book 13
Ryder: SEALs of Honor, Book 14
Macklin: SEALs of Honor, Book 15
Corey: SEALs of Honor, Book 16
Warrick: SEALs of Honor, Book 17
Tanner: SEALs of Honor, Book 18
Jackson: SEALs of Honor, Book 19
Kanen: SEALs of Honor, Book 20
Nelson: SEALs of Honor, Book 21
Taylor: SEALs of Honor, Book 22
Colton: SEALs of Honor, Book 23
Troy: SEALs of Honor, Book 24
Axel: SEALs of Honor, Book 25
Baylor: SEALs of Honor, Book 26
Hudson: SEALs of Honor, Book 27
Lachlan: SEALs of Honor, Book 28
SEALs of Honor, Books 1–3
SEALs of Honor, Books 4–6
SEALs of Honor, Books 7–10
SEALs of Honor, Books 11–13
SEALs of Honor, Books 14–16
SEALs of Honor, Books 17–19

SEALs of Honor, Books 20–22
SEALs of Honor, Books 23–25

Heroes for Hire
Levi's Legend: Heroes for Hire, Book 1
Stone's Surrender: Heroes for Hire, Book 2
Merk's Mistake: Heroes for Hire, Book 3
Rhodes's Reward: Heroes for Hire, Book 4
Flynn's Firecracker: Heroes for Hire, Book 5
Logan's Light: Heroes for Hire, Book 6
Harrison's Heart: Heroes for Hire, Book 7
Saul's Sweetheart: Heroes for Hire, Book 8
Dakota's Delight: Heroes for Hire, Book 9
Tyson's Treasure: Heroes for Hire, Book 10
Jace's Jewel: Heroes for Hire, Book 11
Rory's Rose: Heroes for Hire, Book 12
Brandon's Bliss: Heroes for Hire, Book 13
Liam's Lily: Heroes for Hire, Book 14
North's Nikki: Heroes for Hire, Book 15
Anders's Angel: Heroes for Hire, Book 16
Reyes's Raina: Heroes for Hire, Book 17
Dezi's Diamond: Heroes for Hire, Book 18
Vince's Vixen: Heroes for Hire, Book 19
Ice's Icing: Heroes for Hire, Book 20
Johan's Joy: Heroes for Hire, Book 21
Galen's Gemma: Heroes for Hire, Book 22
Zack's Zest: Heroes for Hire, Book 23
Bonaparte's Belle: Heroes for Hire, Book 24
Noah's Nemesis: Heroes for Hire, Book 25
Tomas's Trials: Heroes for Hire, Book 26
Heroes for Hire, Books 1–3
Heroes for Hire, Books 4–6

Heroes for Hire, Books 7–9
Heroes for Hire, Books 10–12
Heroes for Hire, Books 13–15
Heroes for Hire, Books 16–18
Heroes for Hire, Books 19–21
Heroes for Hire, Books 22–24

SEALs of Steel
Badger: SEALs of Steel, Book 1
Erick: SEALs of Steel, Book 2
Cade: SEALs of Steel, Book 3
Talon: SEALs of Steel, Book 4
Laszlo: SEALs of Steel, Book 5
Geir: SEALs of Steel, Book 6
Jager: SEALs of Steel, Book 7
The Final Reveal: SEALs of Steel, Book 8
SEALs of Steel, Books 1–4
SEALs of Steel, Books 5–8
SEALs of Steel, Books 1–8

The Mavericks
Kerrick, Book 1
Griffin, Book 2
Jax, Book 3
Beau, Book 4
Asher, Book 5
Ryker, Book 6
Miles, Book 7
Nico, Book 8
Keane, Book 9
Lennox, Book 10
Gavin, Book 11

Shane, Book 12
Diesel, Book 13
Jerricho, Book 14
Killian, Book 15
Hatch, Book 16
Corbin, Book 17
The Mavericks, Books 1–2
The Mavericks, Books 3–4
The Mavericks, Books 5–6
The Mavericks, Books 7–8
The Mavericks, Books 9–10
The Mavericks, Books 11–12

Collections
Dare to Be You...
Dare to Love...
Dare to be Strong...
RomanceX3

Standalone Novellas
It's a Dog's Life
Riana's Revenge
Second Chances

Published Young Adult Books:

Family Blood Ties Series
Vampire in Denial
Vampire in Distress
Vampire in Design
Vampire in Deceit
Vampire in Defiance

Vampire in Conflict
Vampire in Chaos
Vampire in Crisis
Vampire in Control
Vampire in Charge
Family Blood Ties Set 1–3
Family Blood Ties Set 1–5
Family Blood Ties Set 4–6
Family Blood Ties Set 7–9
Sian's Solution, A Family Blood Ties Series Prequel
    Novelette

Design series
Dangerous Designs
Deadly Designs
Darkest Designs
Design Series Trilogy

Standalone
In Cassie's Corner
Gem Stone (a Gemma Stone Mystery)
Time Thieves

Published Non-Fiction Books:

Career Essentials
Career Essentials: The Résumé
Career Essentials: The Cover Letter
Career Essentials: The Interview
Career Essentials: 3 in 1

Made in United States
North Haven, CT
30 April 2022